"So why me?"

Rachel lifted her chin. "I've got to have someone impartial on my side."

"Impartial?" he drawled. "Come on, Rachel. You know better than that."

Rachel drew herself up. "One more time, Mr. Cordasic. Do you want the job or not?"

Mr. Cordasic. He smiled. No doubt she knew how hot she looked when she was angry. He masked his very male reaction to her high color and heaving chest by cocking his head. "Before I can make a decision, I need to know if you've told me everything."

A shadow came and went in her impossibly blue eyes. "Yes." She lifted her chin, the way she always did when she was lying.

Some things never changed.

And a fool was born every day.

"I'll take the job," he said.

Dear Reader,

Welcome to my new Romantic Suspense series,
THE CORDASIC LEGACY. When Silhouette Books
asked me to put together a new miniseries, I started
playing the "what if" game we writers often play. Families
often have their own traditions, and we've all heard of
families where there have been generations of doctors or
lawyers. What if there was a family with a long history of
intelligence work? Enter the Cordasic family. Ever since
the American Civil War, members of this family have been
involved in this noble occupation, whether working for the
FBI, CIA, military covert ops, or as a spy. Carrying on this
proud tradition is the Cordasic way.

Black Sheep P.I. tells the story of Dominic Cordasic, the
first family member in decades to have a misstep. His
redemption and reconciliation with the woman who helped
him fail is an intriguing story.

Next up, I'm planning to write the story of Dominic's
brother, Sebastian, a man with a unique condition that
makes him unable to feel. Then Lea, their sister,
is patiently waiting in the wings, insistent that she,
too, has a story to tell.

Enjoy!

Karen

BLACK SHEEP P.I.

Karen Whiddon

Silhouette®

Romantic

SUSPENSE

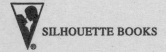

SILHOUETTE BOOKS

ISBN-13: 978-0-373-27583-0
ISBN-10:　 0-373-27583-8

BLACK SHEEP P.I.

Books by Karen Whiddon

Silhouette Romantic Suspense

*One Eye Open #1301
*One Eye Closed #1365
*Secrets of the Wolf #1397
The Princess's Secret Scandal #1416
Bulletproof Marriage #1484
**Black Sheep P.I. #1513

Silhouette Nocturne

*Cry of the Wolf #7
*Touch of the Wolf #12

Signature Select Collection

*Beyond the Dark
"Soul of the Wolf"

*The Pack
**The Cordasic Legacy

KAREN WHIDDON

started weaving fanciful tales for her younger brothers at the age of eleven. Amidst the Catskill Mountains of New York, then the Rocky Mountains of Colorado, she fueled her imagination with the natural beauty of the rugged peaks and spun stories of love that captivated her family's attention.

Karen now lives in North Texas, where she shares her life with her very own hero of a husband and three doting dogs. Also an entrepreneur, she divides her time between the business she started and writing the contemporary romantic suspense and paranormal romances that readers enjoy. You can e-mail Karen at KWhiddon1@aol.com or write to her at P.O. Box 820807, Fort Worth, TX 76182. Fans of her writing can also check out her Web site, www.KarenWhiddon.com.

Chapter 1

"I need you to find my husband's killer."

Dominic Cordasic stared at the shapely blonde behind the polished oak desk. Was she crazy? It had been seven years since he'd last seen her, seven years since she'd dumped him for Evan Adair, and *this* was why she'd asked to see him?

"No," he told her, taking pleasure in the way she narrowed her cat-like blue eyes. "I can't."

"Can't? Or won't?" Rachel Everhart Adair crossed her arms, multiple bracelets jangling. "I'm offering you the opportunity of a lifetime. Media exposure galore. You'll be the most popular private investigator in Las Vegas if you succeed." Despite having spent the last eight years in Vegas, she hadn't lost her Texas drawl.

"And if I fail?" He couldn't resist taunting her, though part of him knew he also jeered at himself.

"You won't." The quiet confidence in her voice stunned him. Was she deliberately reminding him of happier times, when they'd believed in each others' dreams?

No doubt she knew how badly he needed the work.

Still, this was Rachel. The woman with whom he'd left Texas to settle in Vegas, where she could pursue her dream of becoming a dancer. Rachel. The woman who'd broken his heart.

Continuing to study her, he considered. Evan Adair had died six days ago. He'd keeled over in a strip club, cause of death, poison. Like everyone else, Dominic had learned the tawdry details from the television news. The media made everything seem cut-and-dried. Dead man, younger wife, a lot of money at stake. Of course she'd killed him. Suppositions of her guilt were made obliquely, with smug certainty, though the police hadn't charged her with the crime.

"You don't appear too grief-stricken."

She lifted her chin. "I didn't kill my husband. I can promise you that."

No stuttering. The Rachel he'd known since college always stuttered when she lied—was it possible she was now telling the truth? He scratched his chin, holding her gaze. Either that, or she'd finally taught herself to enunciate when lying.

"I'll pay you fifty thousand dollars," she said, her beautiful eyes flashing.

Damn. To distract himself, Dom glanced around her office. Plush patterned carpet, expensive furniture, fancy artwork on the walls. Even her view was top-notch, providing a panoramic look at the strip. From here he could see the distinctive mock Eiffel Tower of the Paris, the glittery Bellagio, and New York—New York's eccentric skyline. Her surroundings showed all the trappings of a wealthy, successful life. Exactly the sort of life he'd left behind when he and Rachel moved to Las Vegas. The sort of life Rachel had never had.

She made a sound of impatience and he focused again on her, ignoring the tug at his heart. She was just as lovely as always, though now she looked a lot more pampered than the young woman who'd once agreed to become his wife. Of course, he'd seen her on TV, but the cameras hadn't conveyed the impact she made in person. Even in her severe black suit she exuded innocence and sensuality, though she acted as though she were completely unaware of that impact.

Dom would bet his last dime that Rachel Adair knew the exact value of using her charms. After all, she'd married one of the wealthiest men in Vegas.

Who had just been murdered.

"Why me?" he asked. "There are lots of other more established private-investigation firms in town."

She bit her lip, and for a moment he thought she wouldn't answer. Then, "Because you're the only one I can trust."

Since her husband had been one of the most influential people on the strip, her words made no sense. "You don't even know me anymore."

"You haven't changed." She held up one perfectly manicured hand, stopping him from speaking. "Oh, I know there have been some problems in your life. I know you've had a few setbacks. But inside, you're still the same man I knew. Rock solid."

Leaning forward, she gave him a close-up view of her

ample cleavage. Deliberate or not, the move caused him to start to sweat.

"Knew." He emphasized the word. "You knew me. You don't know jack about me now."

"People don't change that much. No matter what's happened to you, I believe that. That's why I need you."

Her choice of words had to be deliberate. She probably could guess how often she'd haunted his dreams over the years. But she'd never know how much her leaving had hurt him. That he'd vowed seven long years ago.

When he didn't respond, Rachel sighed and shook her head. Her long blond hair moved in a silky swirl around her shoulders. "Dom, either you want the job or you don't."

Oh, he wanted it. Hell, he needed it. His piece-of-crap private-detective agency was barely making it. He'd just finished up his lone case this month, and he was still working out of his apartment with no staff. At this rate, it'd be years before he could prove to his family that he'd climbed out of the pit he'd dug after Rachel left him. Fifty thousand dollars would go a long way toward achieving that goal.

But more than the money, the benefits he'd reap if he could actually find Evan Adair's killer… That is, if there really *was* another killer.

Personally, Dom had always taken pride in shooting from the hip, being up-front and real. No matter how much trouble telling the truth caused. He'd always believed his honesty had been what made him a hell of a hostage negotiator—until he'd failed, with devastating results. Still, he saw no reason to pussyfoot around now. "Give me a reason to believe you didn't kill him."

"I'm not a murderer."

He smiled. Still no stuttering. "You'll need to do better than that."

"Fine." She got up, walked to the door and closed it. Returning to her leather chair and taking a seat, she took a deep breath. "Evan had some sort of list. I'm not sure whose names are on it, but everyone wants it. The FBI has been investigating—"

He snapped his head up. "The FBI?" His former employer. "Why?"

"They think Evan might have been involved in terrorist activities."

Terrorist activities. He felt like he was standing in the eye of a hurricane, with the worst yet to come. "This list. Tell me about it."

"Evan first mentioned the list when he told me he'd received death threats. He didn't seem too worried, said 'they' were after the list. At the time, he claimed it was simply a list of his business partners. But if he *was* engaged in illegal activities, especially terrorist activities, revealing these people would be explosive. And now Evan's dead."

"You told this to the police?"

"Yes. But they acted like they thought I made up a story to try and get away with the murder." She swallowed, the movement of her slender throat drawing his eye. "Since Evan died, I've been getting threatening calls. The police tried to trace them at first, but they're too short, too random. And I believe they think I've hired someone to make them so that I seem less guilty." She paused, seeming to assess his reaction. "Whoever is making the calls wants the list. I don't have it. I don't even know where it is."

A list. Dom could only imagine what kind of names might be on it. The careers such a list would ruin, the marriages it would destroy if it could tie those named to terrorist activities. A list like that would be very valuable.

"These threats, how specific were they?"

She shrugged, the nonchalant gesture at war with the worry in her blue eyes. "Against me, not specific at all. But lately, the caller has been threatening my son."

Her son. Hearing her say it brought up another old ache. She and Evan had a five-year-old child together.

Pretending he hadn't felt her words like a knife, he clenched his teeth. "Why?"

"Blackmail. He wants the list." Clearly agitated now, she ran a hand through her hair. "Obviously, this must be the same person who killed Evan."

"Why me?" he asked again.

"I told you, I trust you. I don't trust anyone else, not anymore. We've got to find this list before anyone else does. Only once I have it can I protect my son. Will you help me?"

Instead of answering, he crossed to the window, staring sightlessly at the traffic below. "These threats against your son...does the kid know?"

"Absolutely not. I don't want him to be constantly afraid."

"Don't you think you should warn him? Help him prepare, so he can protect himself?"

"He's only five, Dom. Everything has been difficult enough for him, with his father dying. I don't want to make things worse."

The love and worry in her voice brought an ache to his chest. As though doing so could protect him, he crossed his arms and turned to face her. "He'll have to be told."

For one heartbeat she looked as though she might argue, but then she nodded. "You're a professional," she said. "If you think knowing will help protect him, then I'll tell him." She set her jaw. "You'd better not be wrong."

"I'm not." He studied her, deliberately letting his gaze roam over her lush chest, as though he were immune.

"Have you told me everything now?"

A shadow came and went in her impossibly blue eyes. "Y-y-yes," she stuttered.

Some things never changed.

And a fool was born every day.

"I'll take the job," he said.

"Good." She stuck out her hand. "Welcome to the Lone Star family."

Feeling as though he were stepping into an abyss, he reached out his hand. When their fingers connected, he felt his entire world crumble.

Stupid. He gave himself a mental shake. "When do you want me to start?"

Her lips curved. "How about now?"

When she smiled, he felt it like a punch to the gut. Though a lot of what they'd shared still haunted him, he'd somehow managed to forget about the power of that smile.

Throat dry, he stood dumbstruck and tried to collect his thoughts. Finally, he gave a curt nod. "Works for me." He sounded like he'd swallowed a mouthful of rusty nails.

"Great," she continued as though she hadn't noticed. "I'll have a room prepared for you."

"No." Though the blood was returning to his brain, he still felt incapable of stringing a completely rational sentence together. "No room. I'll drive in."

She nodded, though a shadow darkened her eyes to the color of sapphires. "I'd really rather you stay here."

"Why?"

Color staining her cheeks, she held his gaze. "Several reasons. You can search for the list 24–7. And you'll be here the next time someone makes a threat."

Dragging his hand through his hair, he gave her a hard stare. "Why here at the hotel rather than at your house? Wouldn't it be safer there?"

"Lately, we've been staying here." Though she kept her head up, she dropped her eyes.

She'd succeeded in surprising him, something that happened rarely these days. "Why?"

Now, she met his gaze. "I was leaving Evan. Right before he was murdered, I asked him for a divorce. I moved in here rather than stay at the house with him."

He groaned. "Talk about motive…."

"You're wrong. Why would I bother to ask for a divorce if I was planning to kill him? We had an airtight prenup."

She had a point. Still… "And you relayed this info to the police, too?"

"Of course. I have nothing to hide."

Though she didn't stutter, he wondered. But talking to him appeared to have exhausted her. The hollows of her cheekbones seemed more pronounced and there were faint dark circles under her shocking blue eyes.

"Today you're moving out. Back to your house. It'll be easier to keep an eye on you and your son there. We can come back here and look for this list after we finish searching your house."

"I'll go, but only if you stay there, too."

Dangerous. Yet, if he were to be entirely truthful with himself, he'd never purge this woman from his system without a trial by fire.

He could feel his capitulation even as he spoke. "Fine. Why don't you go get packed. On the way to your house, I'll need to swing by my apartment to pick up a few things."

Unsmiling, she nodded. "I'll need some time. I have to get Cole's things ready, too."

"Cole?"

"My son."

Once again, she'd surprised him. "Your son is still here? I'd have thought you'd have sent him off somewhere safe so he couldn't be used against you."

"No," she said. "I'll be back in a few minutes." She started to leave, then paused. "Dom?"

He forced his suddenly tense shoulders to relax. "Yeah?"

"I think you should come up and meet Cole before we go."

Reluctantly, he nodded. He wasn't good around kids, his sheer size seemed to intimidate them. Plus he and Rachel had talked about having children, and meeting the child she'd had with another man didn't rank high on his list of desires.

Still, if he wanted the job, he had no choice.

"Are you ready?" Gazing at him expectantly, she didn't seem to notice his lack of enthusiasm.

"Sure. Lead on." He fell into step behind her.

The exotic scent she wore lingered in his nose as they strode down the hall. Rachel seemed unimpeded by her high heels, even on the thick carpet. Some women couldn't wear the things—they limped around as though every step was torture—but Rachel appeared completely at ease in hers. Without them, she'd be tiny. He remembered how the top of her head used to tuck right under his chin.

She'd never worn heels when he'd known her, claiming they ruined a dancer's feet. She'd changed. Money did that to people, he supposed. While he'd be the first to admit he knew nothing about fashion, even he could tell her clothes were expensive and well made.

During their time together, she'd preferred jeans and soft, well-worn T-shirts. Damn. He had to stop thinking about the past. Or he'd never survive this job.

Seeing Dominic again was agony. If not for the very real threat to her son, Rachel would never have called him. The way he affected her worried her. She'd believed she was over him. He was her past, the past she'd worked so hard to forget. She had to move forward now, focus solely on keeping her son safe and clearing her own name.

To do that, she needed Dominic, the man from her past.

All her life, she'd known only men like him. In fact, her uncles and male cousins in Fort Worth, Texas, were similar. Hard-working, rough talking men's men. They loved NASCAR and football, fishing and sex, and a cold beer at the end of the day. Although her immediate family now consisted of only her mother and her sister, her fraternal twin, her father had been the same when he was alive.

Until she'd met Evan, she hadn't known any other type of man existed. Evan had been their polar opposite—elegant and refined, well-educated and well-spoken. And back then, she'd been an impressionable fool. Until he'd threatened her, she'd believed him harmless.

Rachel sighed. As unsettling as seeing Dom again might be, her former fiancé had better be a damn good private investigator. She needed to find out who'd killed her husband before the murderer came for her son.

"This way," she told him. "Once you meet Cole, I'll pack and then we can get on our way."

He grunted something unintelligible in reply. Her hyperawareness of him made her jittery and overly self-conscious as she led the way to her private elevator.

The thirteenth floor of the Lone Star Hotel was her private floor. Once they'd stepped inside, she punched the button.

"You kept the number." Dominic's face revealed his surprise. "Most hotels simply ignore it."

"Evan's personal joke. While he left it off the public elevators, he kept it for us. Since none of the rooms on the floor are available to customers, no one knows."

He nodded. Wishing the elevator didn't feel so small, she kept sneaking peeks at him, wondering if he felt as confined as she. A big man, he dominated the space without even trying. They waited in silence until they reached her floor and the elevator door opened.

"Mom!" The instant they stepped out onto the carpet, Cole called her. Jumping up and down with excitement at the other end of the hallway, he stood outside the door to their suite with his nanny, Giselle, who'd suddenly quit that morning. Rachel'd had to beg her to stay this last day. She nodded as Giselle slipped past. The nanny wasn't quite brave enough to look Rachel in the eye.

Grinning, Rachel crouched down and held out her arms to her son. He tore off, running straight for her. High heels and all, she caught him mid-jump and twirled him around before wrapping him in a bear hug.

"Looks like you've got that move down." Dom's smile somehow made him look more dangerous.

Kissing Cole's hair, she met Dom's eyes over her son's head. "It's a routine we do. All we have is each other." She let her fierce voice carry a warning. "We won't be separated."

"Wouldn't dream of it."

"This is Cole." She held her breath.

Wide-eyed, the kid stared at Dom.

Dom ratcheted his smile up a notch, turning on the charm. "Hi, Cole. I'm Dom."

"What do you want?" Twisting around in his mother's arms, the boy squinted, studying him. "Are you another policeman?"

"No, honey." Rachel answered before Dom could speak. "He's an old friend from the past."

"Pleased to meet you." Wiggling out of Rachel's arms, the five-year-old walked over to Dom and stuck out his hand, his serious expression far too adult for his years.

Dom shook Cole's hand, equally grave.

"Why are you here?" Cole asked, with the characteristic bluntness exhibited only by small children and elderly people. "Do you want to work at the Lone Star? Are you a valet? You look like a valet, 'specially if you were parking a black Corvette." He regarded Dom hopefully.

"He's none of the above." Rachel ruffled Cole's hair. "Mr. Cordasic is a private investigator."

"Like Inspector Gadget?" Cole inched closer to Dom,

checking out his arms and hands, no doubt looking for all kinds of marvelous gadgets.

"You watch that show?" Dom raised a brow. "That cartoon used to be one of my favorites."

"Me, too!" Cole spun around. "Are you an inspector like him? Where are your gadgets?"

"Sorry, no gadgets." Dom grinned, resisting the urge to ruffle Cole's hair himself. "I'll be doing some work for your mother."

"Can I help?" Cole grinned back. "I know lots of things, like secret hiding places and stuff."

Unsure how to answer, Dom looked at Rachel, who shrugged.

"Sure," Dom said. "Every P.I. needs a good helper."

The little boy's pleased smile faded. "Are you trying to find who kilt my dad?"

Rachel gasped. "Cole…"

"Mommy." Cole waggled his finger at Rachel and gave her a way-too-grown-up look. "I listen real good. Somebody kilt daddy and you want to find the bad man so he can go to jail, right?"

"Right." Rachel grabbed Cole and gave him a fierce hug. "Sometimes, you're way too old for your years."

"Mommeeee." The way Cole dragged out the word made him sound more like an early teenager than a five-year-old to Dom's ears.

Chest aching, Dom wished he could banish the thought that this boy should have been his son. His and Rachel's, not Rachel's and Evan Adair's.

Glancing at his watch, he cleared his throat. "You need to pack. We've got to get going."

"Where?" Cole looked at his mother. "Where are we going?"

"We're going home."

"Home?" His confusion gave way to childlike elation. "Yay!" He took off down the hall, then skidded to a halt. "Is he coming, too?" He pointed at Dominic.

"Yes."

Dom tensed, wondering how he'd react. To his surprise, the small boy seemed pleased.

"Okay." Cole said, beaming.

"Let's get you packed."

"I can do it on my own," he insisted, laughing as he disappeared into the suite.

"What about you?" Dom asked Rachel.

"It won't take me long to get ready. Most of my things are still packed. I can call one of my bellmen to get the bags."

"No need. I'll get them."

They walked to the double oak doors marked Adair and Rachel pushed them open. Indicating a chair, she barely looked at him. "Please, wait here. It'll just take me a few minutes to gather my things. Then I need to go help Cole finish."

Watching her walk off to one of the two separate doorways that must lead to the bedrooms, he turned his attention to his surroundings. The plush suite screamed old-school money, from the heavy cherrywood furniture to the wine-colored damask drapes. In addition to the sitting area, there was a long, gleaming dining table and an antique desk.

A huge console dominated one of the walls. Dom opened the doors, unsurprised to find a state-of-the-art, 50-inch, flat-screen plasma TV.

"Help yourself to the bar," Rachel called out, still in her room. "Cole, are you about done?"

"Yep. I left my suitcase open so you can check it," Cole shouted from his room.

"I'll be right there," Rachel said as she emerged.

He turned to look at her. Anything he might have tried to say stuck in his throat. She'd changed into a pair of faded jeans. The worn material clung to her shape, and the high heels she still wore made her legs look impossibly long. She'd also donned a soft, faded T-shirt.

She looked like the Rachel from his memories, only ten times more beautiful.

His chest ached. Unbelievably, tears stung his eyes.

Rachel shot Dom a surprised look. "What's wrong? You look…uncomfortable."

He shrugged. "Just ready to go."

Before she could respond, the phone on the ornate desk gave one long, shrill ring, then another. A small frown creased Rachel's smooth forehead. "That's an in-house call." She picked up the receiver and answered. The color leached from her face. She slammed the phone down, glaring at it and then at Dom.

"That was him. He said he's tired of waiting. He told me to get rid of you and hand over the list or my son will die."

Chapter 2

Dom caught Rachel's arm before she made it to Cole's room. "Wait. You said the call was in-house. Did you recognize the voice?"

She shook her head, her eyes blazing. Still pale, they looked an even more impossible blue. "Whoever it is uses some kind of machine to disguise his voice."

"But you're certain it's a man?"

Hesitantly, she nodded.

"Is the FBI on-site now?" he asked.

"Yes. I let them use one of the conference rooms for an office. Why?"

"While you two finish packing, I'd like to talk to them."

"They keep to themselves, but maybe they'll talk to you since you used to work with them."

"Maybe." He wondered how much she knew about the turn his life had taken after she'd left. "Where exactly are they?"

"Go to the front desk and follow the signs to the conference area. They're in the Austin Room." Following him to the door, she shut it behind him. He waited until he heard the sound of the deadbolt turning before heading toward the elevator.

Once he reached the ground floor, he had to pass through the gambling area to reach the front desk, the same as in all casinos. The bright lights and noisy slot machines were designed to distract, but he ignored them and headed towards the registration area.

The concierge pointed the way to the conference rooms. Dom had to take another elevator, descend two more floors, and cross a large concourse before he saw the sign for the Austin Room.

Not for the first time he thought how ironic it was that Rachel, a native Texan trying to leave her home, had married the owner of the Lone Star Hotel and Casino.

Without knocking, he pushed open the door and entered the room.

He counted six people, four men and two women, before zeroing in on the one person he knew. A slender, well-dressed man, patrician features giving his face an old-money look, sat hunched over a long table, oblivious to the team bustling around him.

Nathan Frederick, the FBI's golden boy. He'd been the leader of the pack of smug, self-serving bastards who'd wanted Dom fired. Dom wouldn't have been surprised to learn that Nathan had wanted to be the one to personally fire him, though that task had been left to Fred McKay, Dom's old boss.

Nathan looked up and stood as Dom crossed the carpet. "Dominic Cordasic." Smiling, he held out his hand. "How are you?"

"I'm fine." Ignoring the man's outstretched hand, Dom jerked his chin upward. He knew his clipped tone betrayed his dislike, but he didn't care. Nathan had taken no prisoners on his mercurial climb through the ranks. Dom hadn't seen the other man in years and would have preferred to keep it that way.

Finally, Nathan lowered his hand. "What brings you here?"

"Rachel hired me to look into her husband's murder."

Nathan's blond eyebrows arched. "She did?"

"Yes, she did."

The rest of Nathan's coworkers abandoned any pretense of working and watched the exchange with interest.

"I need a word with you." Dom jerked a finger at the others. "Alone."

Slowly, Nathan nodded. "There's another conference room next door." He came out from behind the table. "It's this way."

They didn't speak as they walked down the hall to the next room. Once inside, Nathan took a seat at the oblong table. "What's on your mind, Cordasic?"

Dom closed the door. Leaning against the wall, he crossed his arms and struggled to keep his face expressionless. Just looking at the other man made him angry. This was a long shot. "I want to know what you've learned about Evan Adair. I'll find out anyway, so I'd appreciate your saving me some time. I'd like to clear my client's name ASAP."

"Classified, old chum. You know that. I sure hope you

haven't forgotten everything you learned during your time with the Bureau." Nathan flashed his smug, completely insincere smile. "If you have, then Rachel wasted her time and money hiring you. You're her last hope."

Last hope. Dom shook his head. He didn't want to be anybody's last hope. Hell, he struggled every day to save himself. How could he possibly save anyone else?

Nathan studied him lazily. "You don't look as disheveled as you used to. Have you quit drinking?"

"Eighteen months and counting," Dom shot back. "People change. You should know that better than anyone."

"Yeah, I do." This time the smile was full of malice. "Like your former partner's wife. Have you checked with Lisa lately? She's changed, a whole hell of a lot. Her life went down the toilet after Raymond was killed."

Dom grimaced. Even now, three years later, hearing his former partner's name brought it all back. The grief, the knowledge he'd failed his partner, his best friend, and the longing, the craving, the need to forget.

Dom wanted a drink now more than he had in months.

He shook it off, glaring at Nathan. "Internal Affairs' investigation cleared me of any wrongdoing."

"Yeah." Nathan's low-pitched laugh mocked him. "But you and I both know the truth."

Dom made a jerky move toward the other man, taking a perverse pleasure when Nathan flinched.

"I'd love to be able to press assault charges against you," Nathan said, unable to hide the nervousness in his voice.

Dom flashed a predatory smile, knowing he outweighed the other man by a good twenty pounds. "I bet you would. But I won't give you the pleasure."

Deliberately, he took several deep breaths, using a technique he'd learned in rehab to calm himself. When he had himself back under control, he retreated to the wall and crossed his arms. "Since we're going to occasionally run into each other, why don't we try and keep it civilized."

Nathan frowned. Instead of concurring or even acknowledging Dom's statement, he cocked his head. "Any more questions, or can I get back to work now?"

"Yeah. What about the threats against Rachel's son?"

Nathan shrugged. "I'm inclined to think she's overreacting, or setting up her own scenario. I've heard the woman's a drama queen when it comes to that kid."

Bureaucrats in action. Dom wondered when he'd become so cynical. He eyed the other man. "So you believe she's guilty?"

For the first time since Dom had walked into the room, Nathan's gaze slid away. "Not my area. I'm leaving that up to the Las Vegas Metro PD. What I do or don't believe has no bearing on her case. Some of us learn from past mistakes."

Another not-so-subtle jab. Everyone in the Bureau had believed Dom's drinking problem had been the reason he'd made such a huge mistake and gotten his partner killed.

Blinking, he focused on the other man. "What about this alleged list? What can you tell me about it?"

Nathan snorted. "We're following up on the rumor, but personally I think it's a figment of Rachel Adair's imagination. She's trying to use that cockeyed story to get away with murder."

Dom took another deep breath, hoping Nathan could read the dislike on his face. "Listen to yourself. What do you have against Rachel?"

"I know guilt when I see it," Nathan shot back. "There's nothing personal about it. Not like you. You're the one she screwed over, not me. I can't believe you even considered working for her." Nathan's laugh set Dom's teeth on edge. "You always were a fool, Cordasic. Don't let good looks and a killer body blind you to the truth. The woman's a murderer, plain and simple."

Dom bit back a retort. At least now Nathan had thrown down the gauntlet. "I take it you didn't like the truce idea?"

Nathan merely smiled.

"Looks like we're once again adversaries."

This time Nathan's smile was genuine as he picked up Dom's challenge. "Yes, we are." He pushed himself up, cocking his head as he raked his gaze over Dom. Walking stiffly, he left the room, leaving Dom staring after him

The idea of going home had seemed to make Cole ecstatic, so Rachel was completely unprepared for the somber little boy who waited for her on his bed. His empty suitcase sat open beside him, contents dumped at his feet.

Her heart skipped. "What's wrong?" She knelt down in front of him and hugged him close.

"I'm scared. I don't want to go home." He trembled. "The bad man called again. I heard. Please, Mommy. Let's stay here."

Cole's sudden change of heart infuriated her, though she was careful not to let it show.

"I won't let anyone hurt you, I promise. And you have a real room at our house, not some fancy-shmancy thing like this." She waved her hand disdainfully at the opulent bedroom, which was identical to hers. "All your toys are there—the ones we couldn't bring with you."

Face muffled in her shirt, he shook his head. "Don't care. This is fine."

Rachel tried, but Cole couldn't be consoled. Finally, she started repacking for him, his brokenhearted sniffles ripping at her heart.

When she'd finished and zipped up his bag, she rolled it out and placed the small, green suitcase near her larger pink one. Then she returned and sat down on the bed. Cole had curled into a ball and hidden his face in his arms.

She touched his shoulder. "Are you ready, champ?"

"Not going." His muffled reply was both defiant and frightened.

Before she could reply, someone tapped on the suite door. Sighing, Rachel went back out and confirmed that it was Dom before letting him in. "Cole doesn't want to go." She led him into Cole's room.

"Why not?"

Cole answered himself. "I like it here. This is my bedroom now."

Behind her, Dom gave a loud snort. "Riiight," he drawled. "Every little boy wishes he had a room like this."

At that, Cole raised his head and glared at Dom. "Go away." His lower lip trembled. "You're gonna do that anyways, 'specially if Mommy brings you near our house."

"What do you mean?" Dom asked slowly, looking at Rachel while they waited for Cole to answer.

But her child shook his head and said nothing.

Rachel hated the sharp pangs of worry her son's strange reactions caused. Obviously, Cole knew more than he was telling. Either that, or his overactive imagination had been working double-time.

If she were a betting woman, she'd put money on the first.

She grabbed her son's hand. "Maybe Cole's right. Maybe we should just stay here."

Cole turned his hopeful look on Dominic.

"Nope." Moving forward and ruffling the boy's hair, Dom grinned, knocking the breath from Rachel's chest. "We're going. It'll be safer and a whole lot quieter. No crowds. I can protect you easier there."

"Protect us from the bad man?" Cole asked, tugging on her hand. "Why does he want to hurt us?"

Great. Rachel chewed her bottom lip. The look Dom gave her reminded her she'd promised to tell her son the truth.

"There are bad people out there," she began, stomach in knots.

He nodded. "Like on TV?"

"Right. So Mr. Cordasic is going to help us find out who they are."

Cole instantly brightened. "A bodyguard," he breathed. "Wow."

Dominic frowned. "I'm not—"

Rachel silenced him with a gesture and gave him a look that she hoped plainly asked him to let Cole have his illusions.

"Can we go now?" Cole jumped up and down with impatience.

"Sure." Tucking a wayward strand of hair behind her ear, she picked up Cole. "I'll still have to come in to work every day, you know. Someone has to keep an eye on things."

Dom followed her to the door and grabbed both suitcases. "Don't you trust your general manager?"

She shook her head. "I don't trust anyone."

"Good." He sounded as if he approved, warming her insides. "It's good to be careful, but I don't think the man can run the casino into the ground in a matter of weeks. Let him run the place. That's what GMs do."

"Her," she corrected. "Evan's special 'friend.' That's why I don't trust her."

Looking back and forth between them as though watching a tennis match, Cole tugged at her hair. "Except me, right Mommy? You trust me."

"Of course, sweetheart." She kissed his head.

"What about him?" Cole pointed at Dom. "If you're letting him come with us, you must trust him, too, right?"

"Right," she said. The Dominic Cordasic she'd known had never lied to her.

Dom flashed another devastating smile. "Come on." He tilted his head at the door.

After a second of hesitation, she walked out the door, holding her son. When they finally made their way to the casino's parking entrance, she waved over one of her valets, then looked at Dom.

"I assume we're taking my car?"

"Nope. We're taking my truck."

She thought for a moment. "Cole needs his booster seat. It might be easier to take my car."

"My pickup is a quad-cab. We can put his booster in the backseat. Where's your car?"

"I have a special parking area in the parking garage. The valet can get it." She tossed her keys to the waiting man. "Jason, would you please just bring the car seat from my car."

He bobbed his head and started off.

"While he's doing that, I'll go get my truck." Dom went in the other direction.

Feeling nervous, Rachel held Cole's hand as they waited. She hoped whoever was making the threats saw her leaving and believed she was going to fetch the list.

She noticed that Dom didn't go far. Though he'd parked in the crowded open lot to the west of the door, he'd lucked into a good spot close to the entrance. He drove a Chevrolet extended cab pickup with a short bed.

"I see the parking lot gods still smile on you," she said once he'd pulled up and gotten out of the truck to grab the bags.

He shrugged. "Some things don't change, especially family talents," he told her. "I'm surprised you remember."

Though her face heated, she didn't look away. "How could I forget something like that? Wherever you go, excellent parking spots open up like magic."

Blank-faced, he nodded. "Too bad that kind of luck never translates to something else, like gambling."

"Hmm." She kept her expression serious. "You never know. Maybe you should try the slot machines just to see if that part of your luck has changed. Only try them in someone else's casino."

His short bark of masculine laughter warmed her. She'd always loved his laugh.

The valet returned and handed over the booster seat. As though he'd done it many times before, Dom installed it with a few swift moves. "All ready?" he asked, looking at Cole.

Clutching Rachel's hand, Cole nodded. Rachel started forward.

Dom stepped in front of her and lifted Cole up, then moved aside while she buckled him in. He helped her into the truck and closed the door after her, and she looked at him with surprise. "Thank you. It's been a long time since anyone did that."

"The Texan in me," he drawled.

This time it was her turn to laugh. "The house is in Lake Las Vegas."

He drove west. Though during the last few years she'd ridden in nothing but limos, luxury cars and the occasional expensive sports car, she felt oddly comfortable there with Dom, perched up high and bouncing with each bump as the truck rumbled along.

She fought to keep from glancing at him, alternating between staring out the window and checking on Cole, who was falling asleep.

She felt Dom's presence far too keenly for a woman who claimed to be over him. But truth be told, every time their eyes met, something hot and intense flared through her. The spark they'd once shared didn't appear to have died, at least on her part.

Dom appeared completely immune.

She sighed, unable to resist sneaking another look. He drove easily, one hand on the wheel, his left arm resting on the frame of his open window. He was beautiful, in a masculine and rugged way. She'd bet he had women constantly throwing themselves at him, begging to share his bed. She wondered how often he took them up on it.

Of course, men had always looked at her that way, too, most unable to see past her face and figure to the woman inside. She'd told herself that maybe men thought differently from women. Evan was certainly proof enough of that.

Dom was proof that some men were different.

With Rachel, her stupid emotions always got in the way. The craving Dom induced in her was more than simple lust, more than a lonely woman wanting a hot guy. Always had been. It'd be so much simpler if that was it, if sex was all she wanted from him, the same kind of hot, exciting love-making men claimed to want from her. A peek at the past, a test to show if her memories were truly accurate.

But now, with Dom, she couldn't keep from longing for more. And more was the absolute last thing she needed right now. The one thing she *couldn't* have.

Since she couldn't throttle the craving, the next best thing was to keep Dominic from realizing the depth of her attraction. He'd probably view it as a sort of bitter justice, maybe even a chance to get revenge for what she'd done to him.

If and when she ever reached the pearly gates and had to give an accounting of her life, the worst sin she'd ever have committed would be what she'd done to Dom, the man she'd promised to marry. Even though she'd had no choice, she wondered if even God would forgive such a thing.

Though, in the seven years since, she'd certainly paid the penance.

They were approaching her exit. "Take the next exit."

Nodding, Dom signaled the turn.

The car came out of a nowhere. At first it seemed the limo, long and black with windows tinted the same dark color, would pass them on Rachel's side. There was nothing remarkable about the vehicle—in Vegas there were hundreds, maybe thousands that looked identical.

But rather than passing, as the car drew alongside Rachel, the driver's window slid down. She saw a flash of silver before Dominic shoved her onto the seat.

"Get down," he yelled, seconds before her window shattered.

Chapter 3

Pickup swerving, Dom stomped the accelerator to the floor. "Hang on."

"Cole," Rachel screamed, twisting around to see her son, who blinked sleepily. Strapped in his booster seat, he was a sitting duck. Frantically, she tried to undo the straps. Finally succeeding, she pushed him out of the booster "Cole, get down. Now!"

"Mommy?" Immediately lying flat on the backseat, his blue eyes huge, Cole stared at her. He looked like he wasn't sure if he should cry or not. "What's happening?"

She tried to reach back for him, grunting when Dom pushed her back down with one hand. "Bad men," she told Cole, trying for a calm she didn't feel. The seat still seemed too close to the window. "Can you get on the floor and make yourself as small as possible?"

"Sure." With the agility of his age, Cole twisted himself into a pretzel-like shape and hunkered down.

"Hang on," Dom said again. "The limo's gaining on us."

She glanced at the speedometer. The needle showed their speed to be ninety-five. "How is that possible?"

"I don't know." Making a quick lane change, Dom cursed. "What the hell kind of engine do they have in that thing?"

The entire truck vibrated. Maybe pickups weren't designed to go so fast.

She heard a ping against the truck's metal.

"They're still shooting." Rachel wished she could touch Cole to reassure him. "Stay down, honey."

"Fine," Dom muttered. "If we can't lose them…" He stomped on the brake, jerking the wheel to the right at the same time.

Someone honked and a semi blew by them, close enough to kiss.

"What are you doing?"

"We're on the shoulder now." Dom glanced down at Rachel. "Hold on. We're going off road. This thing's got four-wheel drive. That limo shouldn't be able to keep up in the dirt."

Rachel raised her head to try to check on her son. Dom shoved her back down.

"Not yet." He said. "Cole, stay where you are for now, okay?"

When Cole didn't answer, Rachel felt a flutter of panic. "Cole, are you all right?"

"Can I get up yet, Mom?"

She shook her head. "Not yet."

"When?"

"Not until Dominic tells us it's safe."

Whatever Cole might have replied was lost as the truck's engine roared. They left the pavement, bouncing through the air and landing hard.

The engine roared again as they took off, back wheels spinning, sending up a cloud of desert dust.

"Hang on." Dom flashed a grim smile. "Luckily, I know this area like the back of my hand. Sebastian and I used to ride dirt bikes out here when he visited."

Sebastian. She hadn't thought of Dom's brother in years. A few years older than Dom, he hadn't been thrilled when Dom left Texas so she could dance in Vegas. She could only imagine what he must have said when she'd jilted Dom for Evan.

"Here." Interrupting her thoughts, Dom handed her a cell phone. "Call 911. At least the police can question those guys. Maybe slow them down. That will give us enough time to get out of here."

Pushing up on the seat, she took the phone, frowning. "I don't think they'll believe me. They all know me there after I reported those first couple of threats. They think I'm crazy."

"Try anyway," Dom urged. "Some help is better than none."

He was right. Stomach clenching, she raised her head enough to punch in the numbers and hit send. Nothing. A second later, she tried again, with the same result. Finally, she checked the phone's screen.

"No service."

"Mom?" Cole punched the back of the seat. "Can I—?"

"Not yet." Shaking her head, she looked at Dom. "The guy who called was serious. I've told him several times that

I don't know where the list is, but obviously he doesn't believe me. He must think I'm giving it to you or something."

"Next time he calls, let me talk to him."

She nodded. "Do you think I could get up yet?"

At Dom's nod, she did, one hand clutching the bar on the dash. Squinting in the bright desert light, she looked around them before she handed the cell back to Dom. The dust cloud they were creating was all she could see.

"Are they still with us?"

"I don't know, but I doubt it."

The terrain, mostly flat earth interspersed with cracked gullies and flat-topped mounds, grew rougher. Twice, Cole bounced up, hitting his head on the back of Rachel's seat.

"Moommmmmm," he complained.

"Back in the booster seat, champ," Dom told him. "Buckle in. It's going to get worse before it gets better."

Cole looked at her for permission. When she nodded, he unfolded himself and bounced again, hitting the back door. When Rachel turned to try and help him, he frowned and shook his head. "I can do it," he insisted.

Dom grinned. "He's a big boy. Let him get up on his own." Cole and he exchanged conspirator's grins.

Though she wasn't sure she approved, anything that distracted her five year old from the danger pursuing them had to be a good thing.

Twisted trees and huge cacti continued to flash past.

"Where are we?" Rachel didn't recognize any of the landmarks.

"We're heading up. This side of the mountain isn't developed yet. That limo sure as hell can't follow us there."

"Let's hope not." She looked back. Cole had gotten

back into his seat. He fumbled with the seat belt, shaking his head again when Rachel tried to help.

"I can *do* it." A moment later, the click of the metal sliding into place told her he had.

"Good job." Rachel smiled, hoping she looked moderately composed. If her little boy understood the full extent of the danger they were in, he'd panic. She needed him to stay calm until they got someplace safe.

"We're climbing." Dom pointed to a sign that said No Vehicles Allowed. "It's an old four-wheeler trail. The county closed it after a couple of teenage boys got killed out here."

"Wonderful," Rachel muttered. "Just wonderful."

As the rutted dirt trail went higher, it narrowed.

"We can get up the mountain," Cole piped up from the back seat. "But what if they're waiting for us when we get down?"

He had a point. Cole and Rachel both looked at Dom.

"There's another way down." Dom smiled. "Construction site. They've been doing some mining up here."

He drove like a pro. Of course he did, she thought wryly. He'd worked for the FBI, after all. She blew a kiss to her brave little boy in the backseat. "Don't worry, Cole. If anyone can keep us safe, Dominic can."

Funny thing was, she totally believed it.

Half an hour later, when they followed an old trail down the other side of the mountain and drove safely first to Dominic's apartment, where they called the police, and then to her house, she knew she was right.

When they arrived at the house, Rachel felt no rush of familiarity. She'd never liked the place. Evan had chosen it, purchasing it without consulting his wife. He'd furnished it, too, hiring a sharp-faced woman to decorate the rooms in a contemporary style that left Rachel cold.

She didn't belong here. That statement was overly dramatic, perhaps, but every time she stepped into the pristine efficiency of the granite and stainless-steel kitchen, she felt out of place, as though in a stranger's home. She could no more cook here than she could imagine sitting down to a family meal in the huge dining room with its ornate crystal chandelier.

She wanted warmth and coziness. Evan's house lacked both. As soon as she was cleared of the murder and had dealt with the list, she planned to put the place on the market. Cheap.

Cole had fallen asleep on the long drive over from Dominic's apartment. Now, with Dominic's help, she got him to his room—decorated with brightly colored trains— and into bed for a nap. As Dom followed her silently back downstairs, she felt uncomfortable, on edge.

In the family room, huge, floor-to-ceiling windows looked out over the covered patio and pool area. The pool had been modeled after the one at the Lone Star, only on a smaller scale. The waterfall, Evan's pride and joy, had cost seventy thousand dollars.

Dominic raised his brows. "No staff?"

Lifting her chin, she shook her head. "I sent them all to work at the hotel. I didn't need them here. I hate this place."

He didn't comment. Instead, he strolled around the room, touching nothing. When he reached the windows overlooking the pool, he turned. "Who decorated this?"

She shrugged. "Evan hired her."

"But you had a say in the scheme, didn't you?"

"No." Her wry smile felt weary, even to her. Right now, keeping up the pretense that she'd had a happy marriage was beyond her. "Evan and I didn't share the same taste. He was appalled when I made the mistake of telling him my decorating ideas."

She wiped her damp hands down the sides of her dress. "Would you like something to drink?"

At his nod, she took off for the kitchen, grateful for something to do.

In the home of the man who'd stolen his bride, Dominic watched her go, aching, wondering if he should get out now before he did something so foolish it would defy the imagination.

If not for the limo shooting at them, he could have walked away, but now that he'd seen the truth of the threats, he could no more leave her than he could stop breathing.

He had difficult questions to ask her, difficult for them both. Turning to stare at the pool, he tried to plan what he'd say. A sound made him look up.

"Here you go." Rachel stood in the doorway. How she moved so quietly wearing those high-heeled shoes, he didn't know. How she'd managed to become even more beautiful was another twist of the fates.

"Thanks." Pretending the sight of her didn't make his heart race, he crossed to her, taking one of the glasses from her hands. "We need to talk," he said. "The police are on their way to take our statements about the shooting, but we've got a few minutes before they arrive."

She nodded. "Here or outside?"

The leather couch looked comfortable. "Let's stay in the air conditioning." He didn't mention to her that, until he scoped out the premises, he could do a hell of a lot better job protecting her and Cole inside four walls.

"Have a seat." She crossed the room, high heels sinking into the plush carpet.

He waited to sit until she'd taken her seat. She'd chosen a straight-backed chair and sat stiffly, her shoulders rigid, ankles crossed. The perfect lady.

Except her face and her lush body belied the image. How well he remembered exploring that body....

Damn. Clearing his throat, he took a seat on the couch across from her and dragged his gaze back to her face.

"I have questions." He leaned back, sinking into the soft leather. This piece of furniture was made for relaxing, for lovemaking, and he wondered if Evan and Rachel had ever used it that way. A flash of jealousy had him shaking his head and again he had to force himself to concentrate on the task at hand.

"Personal questions," he emphasized, resisting the urge to put his feet up on the coffee table.

Her sigh was barely noticeable. "Of course. Though I've probably already answered them. Everyone had tons of questions. The FBI, the police, the media. Maybe you should just read their reports."

She might have been discussing the weather, for all the inflection in her smoky voice. This wasn't the Rachel he'd known so well. "Then you ought to be used to answering them by now," he drawled.

"No." For half a second, she dropped the facade, letting

him see the raw pain and exhaustion in her eyes. Then the professional, elegant stranger was back.

"Ask away," she said, hands demurely in her lap, apparently completely unaware of the battle raging inside him.

"The threats you mentioned, and the list. I talked to the FBI. They don't seem to take those seriously."

A flash of bitterness crossed her face. "Did you talk to Nathan Frederick? He used to hang around with Evan before all this. He's a big gambler. I don't like him, and he doesn't like me."

More surprises. "He used to hang around with Evan?"

"Yes." She crossed her long legs, drawing his gaze. "That's why I was surprised when they put him in charge."

"Nathan is SAC?"

She raised a brow. "What?"

"Special Agent in Charge."

"I guess. But since he came here with his team, it's felt like he's in a race to prove me guilty of murder rather than Evan guilty of terrorist activities."

"Interesting. He told me he was leaving you up to the LVMPD."

"Officially, he probably is. Unofficially, however..."

"That's crap." But they both knew neither of them could do anything about it.

"Yeah. And the police take everything Nathan says seriously, so they aren't inclined to believe me about the threats."

Of course they weren't. Even without Nathan condemning her sans trial, like almost everyone else in town, the LVMPD had already convicted her of murder.

She rubbed her palms on her faded jeans, emphasizing the way the denim clung lovingly to her hips, making his mouth go dry. Settling back in her chair, she recrossed her shapely legs, dangling one slender foot in its impossibly high heel.

Again, his pulse sped up. He cleared his throat, bracing himself. "I need to know about your marriage. Were you happy?"

Though her expression didn't change, her posture stiffened. "You go right for the jugular, don't you?"

"I have to ask." He leaned forward. "You left me for him, Rachel. At least tell me you were happy."

She set her mouth in the way he remembered. "You can read the answers to those questions in any newspaper. They've covered this relentlessly."

"I know." He pretended not to hear the plea in her voice. "But I want to hear it from you."

She sighed. "Evan and I were h-h-happy. In l-l-l-love."

"You're lying." He should have felt gratified. He didn't.

Ignoring his comment, she continued. "Then I got pregnant with Cole."

Some perverse part of him wanted to know more. Instead, he filed that comment away for later.

"How did you meet?" He swallowed. "Though this has nothing to do with what's going on now, I've always wondered. I never asked you, and I know what the newspapers have printed isn't true. You never went to fundraisers, so he couldn't have met you at one."

She looked away. "Evan came to one of the shows I was dancing in." Her bright blue eyes met his, clouded with regret. "Remember when I danced at Caesars in Mindlittle?"

How could he forget? He'd been so proud of her. Ruthlessly, he pushed the memories away. "I see."

"He came to all my shows after that. There were two each night. He was at every one of them."

And Dom had worked most nights, oblivious.

"Why did he lie about how you met?"

"Evan didn't want anyone to know I was a dancer."

Past tense. That explained why she no longer danced. He'd searched the cast list of various shows for years after she'd left him, wanting to see her again, even if only as a member of the audience. "Evan was ashamed of what you did?"

She laughed, the low-pitched sound full of pain. "I was his Eliza Doolittle. He wanted to completely remake me. I haven't danced professionally since we got married."

"I'm sorry," he said, meaning it.

She leaned forward. "Let me make one thing perfectly clear."

He nodded, having a hell of a time keeping his gaze away from her softly clinging T-shirt.

"My personal life has nothing to do with you anymore, okay?"

Again he nodded, wondering if she truly believed that. Changing the subject, he asked about Cole. "Rachel, with this crazy person wanting to hurt Cole, have you thought about sending him to visit your mom in Texas? Or maybe your sister in Denver?"

Rising from the chair, she began to pace. Her long-legged stride was still that of a dancer, fluid and graceful. Finally, she stopped. Twisting her hands, she shook her head. "I can't. He doesn't even know them."

Now she'd managed to shock him. What kind of parent distanced their child from her family? "By choice?"

"Not mine. Evan's. He made me cut all ties with my family."

The more she talked, the more he wondered. If anyone ever had a better motive for murder…

"Don't."

Startled, he raised his gaze to her face. "What?"

"I know what you're thinking. Though I had a lot of good reasons to, I didn't kill Evan."

"Sorry." He hadn't realized she'd be able to read his thoughts so easily. He'd have to work on that. He used to be better at hiding his reactions. Out of practice, he guessed. Of course, Rachel had always been able to read him like a book.

"But you've called them now that he's dead, right?"

She shook her head. "No."

"Why the hell not?"

"Too proud," she whispered. "They warned me not to marry him. And I've changed so much, I don't think they'd like me much now."

Everyone changed. But no matter what spark she believed she'd extinguished, he continually saw glimpses of the Rachel he'd known and loved.

Again he cleared his throat, steeling his expression so as not to reveal his emotions. "Rachel, regardless of your rift with your family, if someone is trying to harm your son, you need to send him away."

Rachel stared. "I can't."

"Yes, you can." He crossed his arms. "Call your sister or your mother. Make up. If you don't want to do that, hell, call a friend. Just get Cole out of Vegas."

She lifted her chin, lips pursed. Then the air seemed to

go out of her as she sagged. "You're right. Of course. I'll see what I can do."

The doorbell rang. The police had arrived to take their statements.

Without a backward glance, she left him sitting on the couch and hurried to answer the door.

After she'd finished answering the uniformed officer's questions and left him with Dominic, Rachel went to her bedroom to think. Dominic was right. As much as she couldn't stand the thought of being separated from her son, Vegas wasn't safe for Cole right now. For his own good, she needed to send him away to stay with someone she trusted. And, though they hadn't spoken in years, she trusted her twin sister more than anyone else, besides Dom.

If Jillie wouldn't or couldn't take him, Rachel would have no choice but to ask her mother.

Taking a deep breath, she picked up the phone. Time to end her involuntary solitary confinement.

One of Rachel's biggest regrets about marrying Evan was the way she'd allowed him to cut her off from everything that mattered to her. Her friends. Her work. All in his game plan, she supposed. The violence he'd threatened, the video he'd had taken of her sister walking to class, which he'd used to get her to leave Dom, all had been weapons in the seemingly endless arsenal he'd used to keep her under his thumb.

The only thing she'd finally fought to keep had been her son. Though Evan had wanted her to terminate the pregnancy, she'd refused.

The thought of a baby had been the only thing that had kept her sane through Evan's repeated rapes, and once she'd gotten pregnant, he'd never touched her again. She'd been ready to kill him if he ever raised a hand to their son, but, thankfully, Evan had seemed to accept Cole's presence when he arrived. While he hadn't been a warm father, he'd bragged about siring a son. After Cole had been born, Rachel had let Evan know in no uncertain terms that if he tried to take Cole from her, she'd fight him to the death.

Since the first time she'd held him as a newborn, happiness had been the two of them. She and Cole. Together against the world.

But in concession, she'd had to give up her family. Not only for her safety, but for theirs.

Her mother had eventually stopped calling and asking to see Cole, finally realizing Rachel wouldn't return her calls. Her sister hadn't given up so easily—after all, they were twins, and she'd known something wasn't right. Jillie had finally shown up in Vegas unannounced, just before she'd become famous, and bullied her way past Evan's elaborate lies to see the baby.

But, though Jillie had tried to get her sister alone, Evan had refused to leave Rachel's side, even for a moment. When Rachel and Jillie got up from the dinner table one night, intending on going to the ladies' room, Evan had grabbed Rachel's arm and whispered in her ear one of his barely veiled threats against her family.

Rachel had known what Evan was capable of. Heart pounding, she'd pulled out of his grasp. Hoping her face didn't reveal her horror, she'd sat back down at the table, telling Jillie to go on without her. Despite Jillie's pleas, Rachel had refused to explain, expressionlessly cloaking herself in stubborn silence, while inside her stomach churned.

Rebuffed, her sister had flown home the next morning, leaving Rachel and her miserable life alone. Rachel had not made any attempts to contact Jillie since, watching from afar as her sister became a famous country music artist.

Now, five long years later, because of what Evan had done, she'd had no one to turn to except a former fiancé, a man she'd once loved more than life itself. A man who was now a perfect stranger with bedroom eyes and a body made for sin.

A man who, because of the terms of Evan's will, she could not get involved with—or Cole would lose his inheritance. She could not deprive her son of that.

Even dead, Evan had managed to keep his thumb on her for the next thirteen years.

Now, only her pride stopped her from regaining her life. Her family still loved her—they'd already tried to initiate contact. As soon as word of Evan's death reached them courtesy of the ever-present media, both Jillie and their mother had phoned. Rachel's assistant, still following Evan's dictates, had taken messages instead of putting the calls through. Rachel hadn't thought to tell her to do otherwise. When she'd gotten the pink message slips, she'd been embarrassed and ashamed and had put off calling them back. Now, staring at the telephone in her hand, she wished she had.

Fingers shaking, she dialed Jillie's number from memory. Instead of one of Jillie's vast entourage answering, an answering machine picked up. Speaking haltingly, Rachel left a message and disconnected the call.

One down, one to go. She still had to call her mother. Dialing before she could change her mind, again Rachel reached only a machine. She left a second message, nearly identical to the one she'd left for Jillie, and wiped tears from her eyes.

Having her family close again would be the first step toward having her life return to normal.

Placing both hands flat on her desk, she concentrated on breathing, on slowing her thundering heartbeat. She'd missed her family so much, her sister most of all.

Now all she had to do was hope—and pray—her twin would return the call.

The phone rang a few seconds later. Breath catching in her throat, Rachel answered.

"Thank goodness you've come to your senses!" No greeting, no preamble, just Jillie as usual, jumping right into the heart of things, her voice ringing with laughter and love. "I knew you would, once you got past the initial shock of not being under that man's thumb. How are you, what have you been doing, how's my nephew and when can I fly out and see you?"

When Jillie finally took a breath, Rachel spoke. "I need your help." Briefly, she outlined her fear for Cole.

"Wow." To her credit, Jillie didn't question her or try to discount what she'd said. But then, as a twin, she knew better. "On top of that, I saw on the news that the police suspect you in Evan's death."

"Yes." Rachel took a deep breath. "I've hired a private investigator to help me with that. But Jillie, I need you to take Cole with you for a while."

For the first time since the conversation began, Rachel's words struck Jillie speechless. "Surely, you don't think—"

"That I'm going to prison? I certainly hope not. But I

really think someone is out to get Cole. Even if I'm wrong, I can't risk him getting hurt."

"What about you?" Jillie cried. "What if this same person is trying to kill you?"

"I've got protection." Rachel didn't mention that her protector was Dom. Jillie had always loved Dom like a brother, and the explanations were more than Rachel could handle right now.

Listening while her sister made plans to drive immediately from Denver to Vegas, Rachel smiled. Her world was tilting toward normal.

Finally, Jillie wound down and they said their goodbyes. And Rachel tried to figure out how to tell her son he was going to go stay with an aunt he didn't remember.

Chapter 4

Though the police made a cursory examination of his truck, the responding officers made it clear they believed Dom and Rachel had planned this as a diversion and for media attention, as a way to make her look sympathetic.

When the two uniformed officers took their leave, not only had they insinuated there'd be no report written, but they'd warned Dominic not to contact the media.

Aware he'd get nowhere by arguing and knowing he'd have no success going up the chain of command, Dom gritted his teeth and kept his mouth shut. More unsettled than he liked to admit by their tone, the instant he'd finished and the squad car had driven off, Dom decided to inspect the house. Though life was never so easy, if he could locate that blasted list, he could solve a lot of problems at once.

Was the list paper? A computer disc? Or what? Since

Rachel had disappeared into her room and he couldn't ask her, he prowled the sprawling home, wondering what it would be like to live in such a massive place.

He agreed with Rachel on the decorating—this airy home with floor-to-ceiling windows letting in the sharp Nevada sunlight had been designed for casual, southwestern furniture, not the dark and heavy pieces Evan had chosen.

Working his way through the main living areas, he arrived at a wing that made him feel as though he'd entered a completely different house. The sitting area had been furnished with period pieces—he was no antiques expert, but he thought maybe Victorian. Delicate chairs upholstered in fussy, outdated fabric flanked a claw-footed, equally ugly couch. The dark paneling and heavy drapes were not only expensive-looking but completely out of place. Even the gold-framed artwork seemed to have been chosen for its overstated, in-your-face luxury.

At one end of the sitting room, double doors marked the entrance to yet another domain. This had to be where he'd find Evan's personal office.

Pushing past the heavy mahogany doors, Dom paused and took in the ornately patterned and ridiculously plush carpet. Cherry paneling lined walls decorated with the same type of artwork found in the sitting room. The short hallway reminded him of the inner sanctum of a successful law office rather than the entrance to a home office, which shouldn't have surprised him, as Evan Adair had once been a very successful attorney.

At the end of the hall, another immense mahogany door told him he'd arrived. But when he opened the door he found it only led to another hallway, another polished wood door, unadorned except for a brass nameplate, and clearly set up for effect.

Trying the handle, Dom grimaced. Locked. Apparently Evan Adair had been paranoid, even in his own home. Dom glanced around him, feeling ridiculous. Though there were undoubtedly security cameras, he was here at Rachel's request. Still, he hated the idea of picking the lock to gain entrance to the dead man's sanctuary. Once inside, he planned to do a methodical search. Though this room wasn't where the man had died, the police should have already searched it.

He could ask Rachel for the key, assuming she had one. From the things she'd said, he doubted she did.

Again, he tried the handle. A simple handle lock, which made him smile. He'd always been good with that kind of thing. His brother, Sebastian, had often joked that it was too bad Dom hadn't chosen a life of crime. There were very few locks he couldn't pick.

A few seconds later, the pewter handle clicked and he pushed the door open. As he'd guessed, the room was orderly, polished and pristine, as though Evan would return any moment. The impression was that of intimidating power.

True to the kind of man Evan Adair had been. Dom had seen photographs of him over the years, with Rachel draped over his arm, as much of a status symbol as his Ferrari and Lamborghini. Evan had been tall and dark, aristocratic-looking, despite his cruel mouth. Dom could picture the man ruling his kingdom from behind this huge carved mahogany desk.

Losing Rachel to a man like Evan had been a bitter pill

to swallow. Seeing her and Evan's smiling faces in the papers and on the news over the years had only made things worse. Learning she'd been unhappy was like rubbing salt into an open wound.

Rumors had always circulated around town about Adair's underworld connections. Though the cops had tried, no one had ever been able to pin any illegal activity on the powerful man. Dom suspected anyone who got close died. Either that or became one of Evan's high-paid employees.

Maybe a search would reveal what had made the man tick.

Ten minutes later, Dom realized any thoughts of gaining easy insight into the man had been overly optimistic. He powered up the computer, though he doubted the mythical list would be found on it. A search of the hard drive came up as empty as his physical search of the room had.

Of course Evan had another office at the casino, but Dom was willing to bet that one would be squeaky clean, too. A man like Evan didn't get ahead by being careless. No, his *real* office would be located somewhere else, someplace no one, not even his wife, knew about. If he could find that location, maybe he could find a clue as to the identity of the killer as well as the list.

Dropping into the huge leather chair, Dom rested his elbows on the polished desktop and tried to think. Though no doubt the police and the Feds had already done so, he'd have to search Evan's office at the Lone Star. He also needed to talk to employees, friends, anyone who might know anything about how and where Evan Adair had conducted his true business.

If that list existed, Dom intended to find it.

* * *

When the glowing green numerals on her clock radio showed 2:45 a.m., Rachel abandoned her attempt to sleep. Crossing to her patio, she pulled open the French doors and stepped outside, staring across the immaculate lawn to the pool. The full moon reflected on the smooth surface, making the dark water appear inviting. Though she'd always hated it, tonight even the massive waterfall at the far end of the huge pool looked refreshing.

Though the sun had disappeared hours ago, the warmth of the desert night was perfect for swimming. Maybe if she did a few laps, she could wear herself out enough to go back to bed.

And maybe she could stop thinking about Dom.

Back inside, she crossed to her dresser and opened a drawer, pushing past all the skimpy bikinis Evan had insisted she wear. Hidden underneath his choices, she'd kept her own swimsuit, a two-piece much less revealing and ten times more comfortable. At least the underwire bra gave her some support.

Padding outside to the pool, she grinned, feeling better already. Dom had been right. The walls surrounding the estate gave both privacy and security while the ever-vigilant cameras watched for any interlopers. Since she'd sent the staff to work at the Lone Star, she'd routed the camera feed to the security room there as well. They'd call her and the police if there was an intruder.

Evan might have been paranoid, but he'd been thorough.

With the reflection of a perfect white oval of moonlight shimmering on the inky water like a target, she dove into the pool.

When she surfaced, slicking back her hair, she saw him. Dom. He'd been sitting in one of the lawn chairs in the shadows.

Great. She nearly groaned out loud.

"Remember when?" he drawled. Across the moonlit night, their gazes connected and held.

Without him adding a single detail, she was transported to another time and place.

They'd gone to a party and after returning to their apartment, buoyed by a few drinks, they'd gone skinny-dipping in the building's pool. Flashes of heat and skin made slick by water and lust.

They'd laughed and teased and played, and finally made love on a towel on a lounge chair.

The memories made her ache with need.

Blinking, she swallowed hard and considered pretending she had no idea what he meant. But if she did, she knew he'd probably tell her more than she wanted to hear.

"We were young." She made her voice as haughty as she could, feeling as though she might be treading dangerous waters. "And foolish," she added for good measure.

Instead of arguing, he laughed. The richness of the sound combined with her longing made heat flash low in her belly. When he stood and crossed the pavement toward the pool, goose bumps formed on her skin.

Damn. She wanted to meet him halfway and relive the memory.

Mouth dry, she watched as he dove into the pool, cutting through the water neatly. When he surfaced, he stood a few feet from her.

Mindful of security cameras, of course she moved.

Laughing again, he moved with her, sending water to caress her. He held out one hand. "Would you like to dance?"

She had always loved to practice her dance moves in the pool, using the water's resistance to tone her muscles.

More than anything, she wanted to dance with him now.

"There are cameras," she told him, sounding prim and feeling foolish.

"So?"

She lifted her chin, wondering if she could figure out a way to leave without appearing to be beating a retreat. "My employees are monitoring them."

"Good. I'm glad you have such state-of-the-art security." He pushed water at her, another caress, soaking her top and making her nipples ache.

Deliberately, desperately, she pirouetted backward, trying to shut off her overcharged awareness of him. Another move would take her closer to the steps so she could just engineer a retreat. Then—

He touched her.

Just on her water-slicked arm, a light, nonthreatening slide of his hand. But the shock reverberating through her was enough to make her freeze, heart in her throat.

"Don't." The single word came out a plea, the sound of someone about to be pushed off a cliff.

He cocked his head, the questioning look on his face telling her he didn't understand.

Of course not. After all, she'd been the one who'd jilted him. He didn't know what her husband had done to her. She shouldn't want him now.

"Are you all right?" he asked. The tenderness in his deep voice was almost her undoing.

"No, I'm not." She began wading towards the steps, no longer caring that he'd made her retreat.

Once out of the pool, she grabbed her towel, wrapped it around her waist, and with one last look at the security camera, took off for her room.

Staring after the woman he'd only meant to tease, Dom wondered at her actions. She'd been nervous, afraid. Surely she didn't think…?

Shaking his head and flinging droplets of water everywhere, Dom dove under the water. He'd swim until he was too exhausted to move, then he'd go to his room. Maybe then he could get some sleep and stop aching for something he could never have.

The next morning Rachel was a no-show. Dom followed the sound of Cole's laughter to find them holed up in the child's room. He could understand that she'd want to avoid him. Logically, that would be the smart thing to do.

Of course he only wanted to pursue. The stupid, stubborn part of him refused to pay attention to logic or reason. Something in his nature…

The image of her perfect shape, water-slick and outlined by moonlight, had been burned upon his retinas. Even after swimming for nearly an hour, he'd tossed and turned, haunted by her.

Her shadow dancing and retreat made him acknowledge the flaw inside him—stupid, stupid, stupid—the need to pursue, to hunt, to possess her once again.

Rubbing the back of his neck, he thought of his past and how he'd shamed the family name. Too much was at stake for him to risk losing everything over a woman who didn't even want him to begin with.

"Good morning?" Voice hearty, he poked his head into Cole's room. Here, at least, the mad decorator appeared to have been banished. Bright blues and greens and numerous painted trains combined to make a little boy's hideout. Rachel and her son eyed him from a nest of stuffed animals.

"Hey ya!" Cole jumped from the bed, skidding to a halt inches from Dom. "Whatcha doin'?"

He couldn't help but smile. Though no doubt Cole had inherited something from his father, his facial features were all Rachel.

"Coming to talk to your mom."

Cole frowned. "What about me? Don't you wanna talk to me, too?"

Before he could answer, Rachel shook her head. "Cole, you need to go brush your teeth and get dressed. We've got a lot to do today."

"Really?" Pushing off Dom's legs, he jumped back on the bed, bouncing several times for emphasis. "Like what?"

"I'll tell you when you're all ready." Rachel took his arm, helping him down and steering him in the direction of the bathroom. "You can wear your big-dog T-shirt."

Apparently, this was exactly the impetus he needed.

"Yippee!" Jumping up twice, he hopped on one leg all the way to the bathroom before closing the door behind him.

"Whew." Rachel smiled. "I wish I had that much energy."

Dom regarded the closed door with a mixture of awe and alarm. "Is he always so…?"

"Hyper?" She nodded. "Unless he's tired, yes. Now, you wanted to talk to me?"

Eyeing her kneeling on the rumpled bed, her hair in wild disarray, her pajama shorts riding up her shapely thighs and her T-shirt doing little to disguise the fact she was braless, he realized he couldn't speak. Not with pure lust consuming him.

He could only hope his arousal wasn't too obvious.

"Uh…" He backed to the door, edging around the frame. "I'll let you get dressed. We can talk over coffee when you're ready."

He beat his retreat, furious at his body's betrayal. How could he hope to regain his reputation if he couldn't even control himself around his client?

Twenty minutes later, wearing faded denim capris and a colorful T-shirt, Rachel made her way to the kitchen. Cole ran ahead of her, then back, making circles around her while flying his plastic airplane and making buzzing sounds.

Dom had chosen to sit at the kitchen counter, on one of the bar stools. Just seeing him there, his dark hair highlighted by the morning kiss of the sun, brought a tightness to her belly that she hadn't felt in years.

Cole climbed up beside him. "Do you want some of my cereal?"

"Over here, champ," Rachel interjected, before Dom could answer. "You know you can't eat up there."

"But—"

"Your arms don't reach." She patted his booster chair. "Come on now, eat at the table. Mom wants coffee."

Leaning over to Dom, Cole motioned mischievously. "It's not good to mess with Mommy before she gets her caffeine." His overly loud stage whisper was meant to be heard, but Rachel pretended not to.

She got Cole settled with his chocolate-covered flakes and snagged her favorite mug. Once she'd finished doctoring her coffee with liberal doses of creamer and sweetener, she made herself look at Dom. His nearness overwhelmed her and for a moment she couldn't remember what she'd wanted to say.

He patted the bar stool her son had recently vacated. "Hop up."

She balked, instead indicating the patio outside the breakfast room. Shaded from the morning sun, the little area was a private place, yet she could still keep an eye on Cole. "Let's go out there."

Outside, Rachel took a chair facing the kitchen. Dom stood gazing out over the perfectly manicured lawn, a green oasis in the desert, and the massive pool area, shaking his head. "What a different kind of life you've had."

She knew he meant different from the life they'd planned together. They'd talked endlessly of their future, with the blind excitement of young people in love.

A future that would never be.

When Dom turned to face her, she saw he shared her thoughts.

Unable to tear her gaze away, looking at him filled her only with regret, with sadness. For what could have been and never was. She could imagine some lucky woman, loved by him, cherished. If she let herself, she could even imagine a future together. Kids, white picket fence, the entire thing. All of it. Everything she'd wanted, everything she'd been denied.

Even imagining brought her pain. Now, because she'd been forced to marry another man, she would never have her heart's desire. Evan had made certain of that.

Ah, but looking at Dom—she watched the sunlight dance across his rugged face, marveling that a man could be so beautiful. So unintentionally kind. He made her want things she hadn't wanted in years, things she'd forced herself to forget. Things Evan had taught her could never be.

She'd never know that kind of love again. Evan had taken that from her.

Now, it took everything she had to simply breathe, to exist. She was a widow, fighting for her life. She was a mom—and a damn fine one. She was a businesswoman, keeping the Lone Star afloat and profitable until all this was settled and she could find a buyer. The money from the Lone Star would be part of her son's inheritance. She could do nothing to jeopardize that.

When all this was over, when she'd been cleared of Evan's death—and she would be—she planned to take Cole and disappear. Someplace simple, a small town with clean air, mountains and four seasons. A place where no one had ever heard of her or the Lone Star. Somewhere she and Cole could be free to live a normal life, an ordinary life.

"Have you contacted your sister?" Dom's deep voice brought her out of her thoughts.

"Yes. Jillie's driving down." Rachel didn't bother to hide her happy excitement. "She left Denver yesterday. I expect she'll arrive later today. She's promised to call when she gets into town."

He raised a brow. "Have you told her I'm here?"

"Not yet."

He didn't comment. Instead, he gave her one of his punch-to-the-gut smiles. "I always liked Jillie. I was thrilled when she made the big time. How's Alan?"

"He jilted her the day before their wedding."

Dead silence. She knew Dom was making comparisons. Her face flamed. She couldn't blame him.

"Jillie used to say my karma boomeranged and hit her." This weak sort of admission was the best she could do.

"Hmm." Though he didn't say so, she could tell he agreed. "I'm going to need to go back to the Lone Star," he said, surprising her. "I want to take a look at Evan's office there."

"The police have already been over it with a fine-toothed comb."

"I figured." He sounded unperturbed. "Still, there might be something they missed. I also want to talk to the employees, see if they can tell me anything that might help."

When she started to speak, he held up a hand, stopping her. "Even though the Feds and the local police have already done that."

She nodded. "When?"

"Today. Now. I'd like you to go and show me around. However, I'll have to make the interviews private. If you're at my side, the employees might be less inclined to talk."

That made sense. "What about Cole?" Rachel frowned. "I don't think going there will be safe, but I can't leave him here."

"You don't have someone who can watch him?"

"The nanny quit yesterday." She bit her lip. "Plus, after all that's happened, there's no one I trust. I'll have to bring him with us."

"I don't think it's safe," Dom began.

"I won't let him out of my sight. I refuse to let that—" she tried to find the right word "—that terrorist turn me into someone who skulks around hiding. First off, I'll never find the list if I don't look for it. And until Jillie gets here and takes Cole with her, my son is going to be by my side." Rising, she couldn't resist squeezing his shoulder as she passed. "Thanks, Dom."

"For what?"

"Helping me." Swallowing felt painful, but she continued. "I don't deserve your help."

Whatever she'd subconsciously hoped for, he didn't give it. Expressionless, he only stared. "How soon can you be ready?"

Though she hadn't really expected him to absolve her, his refusal to even address the subject hurt more than she'd thought it would. "Give us an hour," she told him. "Cole and I will meet you by the front door." Back straight, she left as gracefully as she could, feeling his gaze burning into her all the way.

Watching her go, Dom pushed away from the wall and let out his breath in a heavy sigh. So Rachel's twin was riding to the rescue. He'd known she would.

He liked Jillie. Though she looked somewhat like Rachel, her personality was different. She was bubbly, less intense. Alone, hurting, he'd contacted Jillie several times in the weeks after Rachel had jilted him. Something he regretted now. But Jillie had been kind, sympathized with his pain and confusion. For that, he could never repay her. Knowing Jillie and her big heart, she wouldn't expect him to.

If he'd known about Alan, he'd have offered to do the same for her, but people like Jillie always had plenty of friends, and she hadn't contacted him.

For her sake, he hoped Jillie had adapted and recovered better to life without Alan than he had to life without Rachel.

Twenty minutes later, Rachel returned, Cole in tow. She'd changed into one of her power suits, this one bright red, and wore another pair of impossibly high-heeled shoes. With her long hair curling down her back, she looked like an upscale lingerie model. Dom supposed he ought to be used to the clenching of his insides when he saw her, but each time his reaction nearly bowled him over.

"Are you ready?" He looked at Rachel but smiled at Cole. The little boy appeared startled, but then he smiled back with Rachel's achingly beautiful smile. Cole tugged his small hand from his mother's and ran to Dom, grabbing his fingers and holding tight.

"Now we're ready," Cole announced.

Rachel's eyes misted.

Dom hustled them out the door before he said something he'd regret later.

The drive to the Lone Star went much more smoothly and uneventfully than the drive to the house. No limos with crazed gunmen chased them; heck, he didn't even see the same car more than once.

"Pull up to valet," Rachel told him as they swung into the casino's long circular drive. He did as she asked, watching as her employee helped her and Cole from the pickup, suppressing the urge to push the young man away and help her himself.

Once inside, Rachel told the concierge that Dominic was to have free access to everything and anything he might want. Then she turned back to Dom.

"All right." Her voice brisk, she suddenly appeared professional. "I've got some work to catch up on. Cole, come with me. You can play in my office."

The little boy glanced from her to Dom and back again. "But today is my swim lesson."

"I know, but—" She swallowed. "Not today, honey."

To Dom's surprise Cole nodded. "The bad men again, right?"

Rachel opened her mouth, then closed it. Finally, she nodded. "Right."

"Can I play with Sherman?"

"Not today."

Cole looked momentarily disappointed.

"You can play with your race cars in my office." Rachel held out the words as though they were a treat.

Cole took the bait. "Really? Can I set up the track and everything?"

"Of course." She kissed his head. "Let's find out what Dominic wants to do. Then we'll get to work."

"Okay." Grinning, Cole stared hard at Dom. "Whatcha gonna do?"

"I want to explore the hotel." Dom looked past Cole to Rachel. "Show me your husband's office."

Her bright blue eyes flew to his, scalding him with their pain. For the space of a heartbeat she stared at him.

Then Cole, oblivious to the undercurrents, jumped in. "I can show him, Mom. I know where it is." He peered gravely up at Dom. "But I'm not allowed to go in there."

Dom grinned. "Come on, Rach. There might be something important in there."

Finally, she nodded. "It's right down the hall from mine. This way."

Right next to hers? If that was the case, Dom seriously doubted Evan Adair kept anything of interest in there. Too much risk that his wife might find out.

Cole skipped ahead of them down the quiet, carpeted hall. At the end of the hall, in a setup eerily similar to the one at the house, were two massive double doors. The little boy stopped short and turned to look at them.

"You can go in," Rachel encouraged. "It's not locked."

Eyes wide, he started to shake his head, then reached for the handle. Hesitantly, he turned the heavy pewter knob and struggled to push open the door.

Dom went to help him.

Once inside, Rachel propped the door open, as though she didn't want to be trapped in the room. "Ready to play with your cars?" she asked Cole.

In answer, he held up his case of miniature vehicles.

"Good. Why don't you go over there and play for a few minutes." She pointed to the far end of the office. Expression dubious, the little boy went, standing awkwardly next to a large, round table and shifting his weight from foot to foot.

Dom saw the problem immediately. Crossing the room, he crouched down in front of Cole. "What's the matter? Afraid to touch anything?"

Mutely, Cole nodded.

"Don't worry." Dom gripped the kid's shoulder, steering him gently towards the table. "We've got new rules now. You can touch whatever you want."

"Really?" Cole looked at his mother.

"Really." Rachel nodded. "You can even drive your cars on the table."

Once Cole was happily playing, Dom retreated back to

the area near the desk, where Rachel waited. She looked so grateful for his interference, Dom's chest ached.

To keep himself from touching her, he dropped into the huge leather chair behind the equally massive desk. Then, clearing his throat, he spoke quietly so her son wouldn't hear. "I don't want him to see me search the office."

"Of course not." She glanced at Cole. "Knock yourself out searching, but like I said, the police have already been over everything."

Marching over to her son, she bent over to speak to him, giving Dom a fantastic view of her trim backside. When she straightened, she held several of Cole's cars in one hand. With the other, she took Cole's hand.

"We'll see you later," she said, giving Dom an impersonal smile.

As she started to walk off, Evan's phone rang.

Chapter 5

"Evan's dead." Rachel stared at the phone. "No one should be calling that number now."

Dom placed a steadying hand on her shoulder. "Are you going to answer it?"

"I—" Wincing, she let go of Cole's hand and reached for the receiver. "Hello?"

"I need the list." The same voice as before.

"Look, I've been trying to tell you, I don't have it. I don't know where it is. Give me time to find it."

"I don't have time. The list or your son."

"I can't give you what I don't have." Desperation made her voice sharp. "Give me a week."

"Two days."

"Four." Was she crazy, trying to barter with a madman?

"Forty-eight hours. Or your son dies." The caller hung up.

"That was him," she whispered to Dom, glancing at Cole. "I want to know who he is." Furious, she swore under her breath. "Since he knew we were in here, he's got to be close, watching us. I don't want that SOB anywhere near my son."

"We'll find him," Dom promised. "If he's here, at the hotel, he's bound to make a mistake."

"He's given me two days to come up with the list."

Dom cursed under his breath. "We need more time."

"I know." Straightening, she took a deep breath. "We've got to find it, Dom."

"You go through your records, looking for a clue. I'll search here."

"Then?"

He shrugged. "Then we'll play it by ear. We can get a lot more done now that he's temporarily lifted the threat."

"I'm ready," Cole interrupted. "Can we go now, Mommy?"

"Of course." Engineering a smile for her son, she gave Dom a worried look over the top of Cole's head. "I'll be in my office if you need anything."

"Wait." Dom touched her shoulder. "If I'm ever going to find that list, I need to know where Evan went the day he died and who he saw. I especially need to find out where else he might have done business."

"Like another office?" She shook her head. "As far as I know, Evan worked here or at his office at the house."

"What about lovers?"

Rachel shot him a warning look. "Later, when there are no little ears."

Cole tugged on her hand. "Come on, Mom."

"Just a minute." Redirecting her attention back at Dom, she spoke firmly, with a confidence the phone calls hadn't entirely banished. "As to all th-th-th-th-the other information, I have n-n-n-no idea. Evan and I weren't—" she darted a quick glance at her son "—close."

Despite the telltale stutter, Dom found himself wanting to soothe the flicker of panic he saw in her eyes. "No worries. Since I'm sure it's all in the police report, I'll probably head down to the station later and take a look."

"Why don't you call one of your contacts at the LVMPD and get him to fax it?"

It dawned on him that she had no idea the hell his life had been since she left. "I don't have any contacts at Las Vegas Metro, not anymore. Not since I left the FBI."

Cole tugged his hand from Rachel's. Frowning, she watched as he chased a car down the hall. "Dom, why'd you leave the FBI, anyway? Even when we were in college, that's all you ever wanted to do."

The old hurt stabbed him. Ruthlessly he pushed it away.

"I was fired from the Bureau, Rachel. After what happened, just about no one in law enforcement will have anything to do with me. People talk."

She shifted her weight, her expressive face telling him she wasn't sure if she should ask. "What happened, Dom? I know your partner Raymond died—it was on the news— but what really happened?"

He answered without inflection, as though the words weren't a fresh knife wound directly in the gut. "A hostage situation went bad. A woman and two kids died while I was trying to talk the man into putting down his weapon. But he killed his wife. Raymond ran in to save the kids. I was too slow to stop it. The perp shot him—and the kids—before a SWAT sniper took him down."

He took a deep breath. "I made a mistake and lost not only the hostages but my partner. He was thirty-four years old. He had a wife and children, Rachel."

"But Dom, what that gunman did wasn't your fault. You did the best you could."

He refused to let her absolve him.

"It *was* my fault. I'd been drinking the night before and I was tired. Not focused. Internal Affairs did their usual investigation, cleared me of all wrongdoing. But *I* knew, and all the other guys knew. I failed Ray. Failed that poor woman and her children. I started drinking more heavily after that, Rachel. Lost my job. My grandfather disowned me—I sullied the Cordasic name."

She blinked. "But you don't drink. I haven't seen you drink since you've been here."

"I'm sober now. Have been for eighteen months."

"And your grandfather?" She knew how much Phillip meant to him. "Has he forgiven you?"

"No." He shrugged, trying to pretend he didn't care. "He says I've got to prove myself to him. Redeem the smear I've put on the family name."

Cole darted by, making a buzzing sound as he crawled under Evan's desk.

Rachel's sapphire gaze never left his face. "Screw the Cordasic name. Forget Phillip, too, for that matter. Dom, a mistake is a mistake. I'm sure they didn't blame you." The intensity in her husky voice made him grit his teeth as raw emotion flooded through him.

Too much, too soon, too fast.

"Maybe not." His emotionless tone was back. "But LVMPD won't work with me. Anything I do, I do on my own."

"If there's anything I can do to help…" Leaning forward, she appeared to be wavering, about to kiss him. His heart stopped, his breath caught in his throat.

"Ahem." Someone cleared his throat from behind her, making her jump. She moved away, her face flushing.

Nathan Frederick stepped into the room.

"What's going on here?" He looked from Rachel to Dom and back again before settling on Dom. "What are you doing, snooping around Evan Adair's office?" He sounded defensive—and furious.

Dom smiled. "Maybe I'm interviewing for the position," he said lightly.

Rachel straightened, but didn't contradict him, a nice gesture for which he made a mental note to thank her later.

Nathan's black look and scowl made Dom laugh.

Lip curling, Nathan glared. "You know, Cordasic, you're making me regret allowing you on board here."

"*Allowing* me? On board?" Dom raised a brow, taunting the other man. "I don't work for the Bureau anymore, remember?"

"Agent Frederick." Rachel's soft tone was wrapped in steel. "Dominic works for me. This is still my hotel and I say who's allowed where and when."

"Only until you go to prison," Nathan snapped. "And we both know that's only a matter of time."

"I'm going to have to ask you to leave."

Making an obvious attempt to rein in his anger, Nathan

swallowed. Shooting Dom another black look, the FBI agent stalked from the room.

"Wow." Rachel sounded winded. "That was weird."

"To put it mildly. Why'd you do that?" Though he voiced the question as though only mildly curious, Dom really wanted to know.

She shrugged, avoiding his gaze. "He's annoying."

"I'm afraid you've made yourself an enemy," Dom said. "Nathan Frederick doesn't forgive or forget easily."

Expression calm, Rachel shrugged. "Maybe now he'll give me a break."

"A break?"

Still she looked everywhere but at him. Eyeing her son, who played intently under the desk, accompanying himself with his buzzing noises, she leaned in and whispered. "He wants me to sleep with him. He's been dropping hints since the day after Evan's body was found."

Even for a weasel like Nathan, his timing sucked. "Your husband's only been dead a week."

"Thank you." She sounded grateful—and faintly surprised. Though that shouldn't have rankled, it did.

When she once again met his gaze, the professional, pleasant Rachel had returned.

He felt an instant of crazed desire, wanting to yank her up against him and claim her lips, to kiss her senseless like he had in the old days. She wouldn't look so untouchable once they were through.

But then he'd be just as bad as Nathan. Like the FBI agent, Dom had no right. Not anymore.

"Dom?" Her hesitant tone brought him out of his

thoughts. "Earlier, I lied. When I told you I didn't know anything about Evan."

Since her stuttering had given that away, he already knew, though he held his tongue and waited.

With another quick glance at Cole, she nodded. "You asked about lovers. Evan had affairs. Lots of them. He delighted in parading his bleached-blond bimbos in front of me."

"Why?" The word slipped out before Dom could think. "Why would any man do that to his wife?"

"Evan wasn't just any man. He was Evan Adair, high-rolling casino owner and self-styled playboy. He told me he got bored easily. I…" She swallowed, before lifting her chin and continuing. "I bored him."

"Did you tell the cops that?"

"Of course. They already knew. Everyone who has ever hung around here on a regular basis knows about Evan and his little flings."

Dom groaned. "Listening to you makes *me* want to kill him. Rach, do you realize with every word you speak about him, you build a better case against yourself for his murder?"

Her grim nod told him she did. "I can't do anything but tell the truth. I've never been good at keeping track of lies."

"You always stammer." Unbidden, he remembered when she'd told him she was leaving him for Evan. She'd stammered so hard when she'd tried to explain why she could barely get the words out. And he, fool that he was, had been so devastated that he'd believed she was lying to spare his feelings, when he should have questioned what she was lying about.

Pushing the memories away, he asked for specifics. But

other than what she'd seen with her own eyes and the constant slew of rumors and gossip, Rachel knew very little about her husband's activities outside the Lone Star. The only business associates she could name were the ones who frequented the casino. She couldn't even name any of Evan's personal friends, assuming he'd had any.

"Any more questions?" She shifted her weight uneasily. Cole had come out from his hiding place under the desk and resumed buzzing in circles around the room.

"Nope." Dom shook his head.

"Then I'll leave you to the rest of your search." She looked him over with a detached smile. "You should know I've searched this place top to bottom. The house, too. If there actually is a list, I don't know where Evan might have hidden it. I've gone through every CD, computer disk and file folder."

With a quick wave, she snagged her son on one of his runs by. "Come on, Cole. Let's go." With a small wave, they left.

Dom found himself staring at the doorway where she'd vanished, wishing he knew what she was hiding and why. And wishing he could stop drowning in memories.

Damn, he'd hoped the connection he'd always felt to her would have vanished by now. He'd always told himself she'd killed it when she left him. Of course, he'd managed to convince himself of a lot of things. Like making himself believe he could love anyone else as much as he'd once loved her.

Once being the key word. He needed to remember that.

Rachel Adair. The woman his family viewed as the instrument of his downfall. His grandfather Phillip, the patriarch of the Cordasic clan, had loved Rachel before the breakup, even making a point to spend time alone with her. Seb had joked that Rachel's defection had hurt Phillip as much as Dom.

Speaking of his family—it had been a few weeks since he'd spoken to his brother, Sebastian, or his sister, Lea. Ever since Phillip had disowned him, Dom had made it his goal to try and regain favor.

Every time Dom spoke to Sebastian, he asked if their grandfather had forgiven him. The short answer was always *no*. But now Phillip, eighty-six and ill, was dying.

Yet even with his time on earth numbering in months, the old man refused to see his middle grandchild, unable to forgive Dominic for sullying the family name so long ago. No amount of reasoning or cajoling would make him change his mind. He'd only repeated his message to Dominic—prove to me that you have the right to rejoin this family, that you're worthy of your inheritance and will carry on the family's legacy of service to our country.

Dom pretended not to care, but his grandfather's rejection was the one thing that spurred him to succeed in turning his life around. Since his father had died when he was small, Phillip had been the father figure for Dom, Sebastian and Lea. Stern and regimented as the old man was, Dom had never thought he'd utterly withdraw his affections as he had. Phillip's explanation, given through Sebastian, had been that he believed in practicing tough love. Once Dom had proved he'd truly changed, Phillip would welcome him back to the family fold.

Dom didn't understand what else he had to do to prove this. He'd cleaned up his life, gotten sober and started his own business. What more did Phillip want?

Sighing heavily, Dom pulled out his cell and speed-dialed the number.

Sebastian answered immediately, almost as though he'd been expecting the call. "Nothing's changed here," he said, issuing the greeting in his clipped, emotionless tone.

Grinning, Dom told him he'd accepted a big case, omitting the fact that his client was Rachel. Though Sebastian had never judged him, Dom didn't want his brother to think he was falling back into his old habits.

"Need any help?" Seb asked. When Dom told him not yet, his brother made him promise to call if and when he did. Dom smiled again. Despite the lack of warmth in Seb's voice, which was beyond his brother's control, Dom knew that down deep, where it mattered, his brother loved him. For Sebastian, Dom would go to hell and back, and vice versa.

Sebastian was currently between assignments, on enforced medical leave. He said he needed to decide whether he should do something other than Special Ops for the military. After Seb had been captured, tortured then released in Iraq, they'd offered him an honorable discharge, which he claimed to be considering, but he often complained to Dom that he found civilian life dull.

Typical Cordasic.

"I'll call you soon." Dom hung up, wondering if his brother would ever regain his true personality. He hadn't been the same since his rescue from enemy imprisonment. Though Seb refused to talk about what had happened there, something had been done to him, some kind of experiment that had left Seb unable to feel.

Though Dom knew his brother's life must be hell,

there'd often been times when Dom wished he could be like him. Being around Rachel now, wanting her despite everything, was one of those times.

Once inside her office, Rachel closed the door behind her. How she wished she could find a spare key to her dance studio. One of Evan's petty pleasures right before he died had been denying her access to her private dance studio. He'd had the place locked up tight, making her watch while he flushed the key down the toilet.

After his death, she hadn't had time to call a locksmith, though she'd have to do so eventually. The humiliation of having to break into her own dance studio was bad enough, but the gossip that would follow would be hurtful.

Even Dom would eventually know. She hadn't meant to hide things from Dom, but some truths she didn't want to share. Like how her husband had treated her.

Heart heavy, she crossed the plush carpet to her chair. A simple, ergonomic design, she loved the way it felt. One of the first things she'd done after Evan's death had been to move out the elaborate leather monstrosity he'd insisted she use.

From the tiniest of changes, she suddenly, fiercely, wanted her pre-Evan life back. She missed her family. Missed her sister's rich laughter, the sharing of clothes, gossiping late into the night. She missed the rich scent of her mother's cooking and the feel of her ample body when she enfolded Rachel in a hug.

She'd taken one step toward regaining her life, speaking to her sister. All apparently forgiven, Jillie was on her way to Vegas, driving to the rescue.

Would her mom forgive so easily? Rachel had hurt her

badly, she knew, and though she'd had good reason for cutting her out of her life, her mother didn't know that. Now, finally, Rachel could tell her the truth.

Before she lost her nerve, she grabbed the phone and dialed the number.

Busy. Blinking, she placed the phone back in the cradle.

"Mommy, do you like Agent Frederick?"

Surprised, Rachel looked at her son. She'd better be careful of what she said to him about authority figures. "He's okay. Why?"

He peered at her over the top of his milk glass, wiping away his milk-moustache with the back of his hand. "Because I don't. I think he likes you." He took a deep breath. "Are you going to be his girlfriend?"

Ruffling his unruly hair, she fought to keep from laughing. Cole had mastered the art of the big-eyed, innocent stare. "No, honey. He's here because of his job, nothing more."

"Good." Cole crossed his skinny arms. "He reminds me of some of Daddy's mean friends."

This surprised her. Especially his use of the word *mean*.

"Why do you think that?" She kept her tone unconcerned, not wanting to upset him. "Has Agent Frederick said or done something mean to you?"

"No." Cole grimaced. "He told me to keep out of his way, that's all."

Relief flooded her. "Were you bothering him when he was trying to do his job?"

"No." At her questioning look, he grinned. "Maybe a little. I want to know what a real FBI agent does."

"You shouldn't bother any of them while they're trying to work."

"Oh, I don't." He pressed his lips together, hard.

"Maybe you could ask him about his job when he's not busy."

"I guess." Cole didn't sound convinced. "But I already tried that. He doesn't like kids. He told me so. I waited until he was eating lunch out by the pool. That's when he told me to stay the h-e-double-l away from him."

"Really?" Her brows rose. Maybe she and Nathan Frederick were due for another talk. No one had the right to swear at her son.

"What about Dom?" Cole's innocent blue eyes sparkled. "Do you like him?"

Good Lord. She needed to tread carefully. "He's an old friend." Hoping her nonanswer would satisfy him, she pointed to his cars. "Aren't you going to set up your racetrack?"

He shook his head. "I want to go outside and play."

"It's going to be hot."

"So? It's always hot."

He had a point. She settled on a compromise. "How about we swim later today, once we get home?"

He scrunched up his nose. "I want to swim here. There are other kids to play with. But no lessons. I don't want to take any more swim lessons, okay?"

She laughed. "No more lessons for now, silly. But we need to wait to swim until we get home." Despite the two-day respite she'd been given, she still wasn't sure the Lone Star pool would be safe for Cole.

She pointed to his cars. "If you'll play while I finish working, I've got a few more things to do. On the way home, we'll stop and buy a new float, okay?"

Nodding, he immediately refocused all of his attention on his toys with all the intensity only small children can muster.

Once he finished searching Evan's office, Dom debated his next move. He could find Rachel and start searching for the mythical list. Or, he could take a few minutes of downtime and try to come up with some sort of plan. He hated feeling so shaky, as though he were standing on a crumbling cliff in the middle of an earthquake. Not for the first time, he wondered if he'd done the right thing taking this case.

Yet if there was any case that would catapult him back to instant respectability, this was the one. If he wanted to see Phillip again before he died, he had no choice but to continue.

Dom snorted. Who did he think he was fooling? He'd taken the case because Rachel had asked him.

Calling himself every kind of fool, he strode to the elevators and punched the button marked Casino. Once there, he wove his way through slot machines, past the poker tables, and headed directly toward the bar. Without taking time to think, he ordered a beer.

The bartender brought a frosty schooner, placing it in front of him. Dom slid a five across the counter and wrapped his hand around the sweating glass.

Amazing how some things would always seem familiar.

Suddenly, he couldn't breathe. The Lone Star seemed stifling, walls and crowds and noise all closing in on him.

Leaving the beer untouched, he turned and headed back the way he'd come, pleased he'd been able to resist that temptation, at least.

The caller had given Rachel forty-eight hours. He wouldn't make a move now, knowing she didn't have the list.

Plus Rachel and Cole were working in her office, under the watchful eye of Lone Star security. They'd be fine alone for an hour or so.

He headed outside to the parking garage and climbed in his pickup. Putting the truck in drive, he took the shortest route to his apartment, needing the familiar. He might not own a lot, but perhaps going home would make him feel as if he stood a chance of regaining control of his life.

But his apartment felt sterile and empty, devoid of anything even remotely resembling a home. He thought of Rachel's beautiful yet austere house in the desert and grimaced.

Were they both really such lost souls?

Unsettled and unable to stay at his own home, he got in his truck and began to drive aimlessly. Finally, he found himself on Stewart Avenue, right in front of the Las Vegas Metropolitan Police Department building. Once, he'd had quite a few friends inside. Now? He simply didn't know. Times changed and people changed, and if there were any who still held his past against him, he supposed he didn't care.

He needed info on Evan Adair. He could put in a public information request and get what they had on the crime scene.

Why not?

As he pulled into the lot, a spot opened up close to the entrance.

Nerves jangling, he climbed from his truck. The short walk to the entrance felt like a condemned man's walk to the gallows.

Once inside, the process went smoothly. The woman on duty at the window didn't know him and handled his request efficiently and impersonally. Carrying his folder to one of the uncomfortable hard plastic chairs, he began to read, beginning with the official police report.

The details of Evan Adair's death sent a chill of foreboding up Dominic's spine. Though the diligent media had reported the man had been poisoned, the autopsy report revealed traces of ethylene glycol, an extremely toxic chemical commonly found in antifreeze. Someone had apparently been slipping it into the man's food and drink.

Usually poisoning was done by someone close to the victim. Several people had gained notoriety lately by killing their spouses the same way. The profilers agreed that this was mainly a woman's method of murder, which was why Rachel was their chief suspect. Actually, Rachel was their *only* viable suspect. Every aspect of the investigation appeared focused on building a case to charge her with murder.

Even Dom had to admit it all seemed pretty cut-and-dried. She had motive times ten. Truth be told, he wouldn't blame her for killing the man.

But she'd hired him to prove she hadn't. Why would she do such a thing if she was guilty? Unless she was using him to throw up a smoke screen, with the goal of distracting both the police and the various pundits who had already proclaimed her guilty.

He continued reading. Though the will had been sealed, the attorney had released the fact that Cole—a five-year-old boy—had inherited everything. Now Rachel claimed her son was in danger.

These notes stopped Dom cold. Though he couldn't wrap his mind around the notion of Rachel as a murderess, he wouldn't have believed she'd jilt him seven years ago, either.

The report said nothing overtly. But Dom knew how authorities thought.

Did they truly believe Rachel was a danger to her own son?

Chapter 6

Already pacing impatiently in the hotel foyer, Rachel jumped when her cell phone rang.

"Jillie?"

"I'm almost there." Despite the twelve hour drive, her sister's voice still sounded unflaggingly cheerful. "Though I'm stuck in traffic on the strip."

"Crud," Rachel groaned. "I meant to direct you a different way. Only tourists take that route. The rest of us go back roads."

"Now you tell me."

"Where are you now?"

"I can see the Paris."

"Not too much further. When you get to the Lone Star, pull right in front and let my valet service park your car."

Closing her cell, Rachel wanted to dance with excitement.

"Mom?" Cole stared up at her. "Why are you laughing?"

She wasn't laughing, she was grinning from ear to ear. "Come on, son." Grabbing his hand, she pulled him along with her. "Let's go wait for your Aunt Jillie."

A few minutes later, Jillie pulled up to the front door in a low-slung, convertible sports car.

"That's a Bentley Continental GTC!" one of the valets said, sounding awestruck. "Those suckers cost around $190,000."

Rachel had to admit it was an awesome car. While Rachel had no idea how much chart-topping country singers made, she knew it had to be substantial. Jillie alternated between two homes, one in Denver and the other in Fort Worth. She also kept an apartment in Nashville.

The car suited Jillie. Low slung and powerful, dark and dramatic, it screamed of expense, luxury and secrets. Rachel couldn't help but wonder how much her twin had changed since the days they'd been fused at the hip.

Hopefully not too much.

"Jillie!" She waved, jumping up and down.

Jillie waved back. Squealing with joy, she barely let the valet open her door before taking off and flinging herself at Rachel.

"I have so missed you." Rachel hugged her back. "You have no idea how much."

"Really?" Jillie pulled back, her expression troubled. "Then why did you work so hard to keep us away?"

"Long story."

"I've got time."

"Yeah." Rachel shook her head. "And I will tell you, I promise. But first, come meet Cole."

"Little Cole? Baby Cole?" Jillie shrieked again, scooping up the awestruck little boy into her arms. "You've gotten so big!"

"You look just like my mommy." Eyes huge, he looked from Jillie to Rachel. "Except you've got more hair."

They all laughed. Rachel and Jillie did look alike, though not enough that Rachel was ever mistaken for her famous twin. Cole squirmed, trying to peer over Jillie's shoulder as the valet climbed in her Bentley.

"I want your car." He pointed, leaning to watch as the valet drove it away. "It's the Batmobile!"

"Really?" Jillie kissed his cheek before setting him back on his feet. "And here I thought all along I had bought a Bentley."

Linking her arm through her sister's, Rachel tugged Jillie toward the door. "Come on inside in the air conditioning."

"Great. It's awfully hot here." Jillie kept up a steady stream of chatter as they strolled past Reservations toward Rachel's private elevator.

"Is that the only bag you brought?" Rachel eyed the medium-sized carry-on.

"I travel light." Grinning, Jillie glanced around the ornate lobby. "You've upgraded this place since I was last here."

"Evan did massive renovations a couple of years ago."

"Well, it looks absolutely fabulous. In fact—" Jillie stopped mid-sentence, freezing in her tracks. "Is that…?"

Rachel followed the direction of her twin's gaze. Dom had just come around the corner from the coffee shop and stood, watching them approach.

"Dom!" Cole yanked his hand from Rachel's and tore off, slamming into Dom's legs.

"Rachel?" Jillie frowned. "What exactly is going on?"

Before Rachel could answer, Dom came over and pulled Jillie in for a hug. "Great to see you again."

"Uh, yeah." Jillie glanced from Rachel to him, then back again. "I'm guessing this is part of your long story?"

"I told you I hired a private investigator." Rachel smiled, feeling better than she had in days. "Let's get a cup of coffee and go up to my room. We can talk in private there."

With Cole skipping ahead, they did exactly that. When Dom tried to hang back, Jillie would have none of it.

"You, too," she ordered. "I'm dying to hear your side of this story."

Rachel heaved a sigh and shrugged. "Dom, you might as well come. You know how Jillie is."

"That's right." Jillie marched on ahead, trying to keep up with Cole. "I'm like a bloodhound. I won't rest until I've sniffed out all the answers."

"Woof-woof," Cole barked. "I wanna be a blood-hound, too."

Jillie laughed. "Okay, honey."

"You know what?" Rachel called after him. "It's just about time for your nap."

Once they reached the suite, Rachel carried Cole into his bedroom and tucked him in bed, Jillie close behind.

"Get some sleep, now." Rachel kissed her son's cheek. "I promise we won't do anything exciting without you."

He nodded, his eyelids already drooping.

"See you later, little man." Jillie kissed him, too, earning a sleepy smile.

Linking her arm through Rachel's, Jillie led the way back to the living room, where Dom waited.

As usual, the mere sight of him, this time reclining on her buttery leather chair, made Rachel's heart beat faster and her mouth go dry.

As if she knew, Jillie squeezed her arm. "I want to hear everything," Jillie announced, dropping down onto the sofa. "Starting with what that bastard Evan did to make you cut off all ties with your family."

So Rachel told her, though she omitted what Evan had done to make her break off the engagement with Dom. She saw no sense in letting Dom know the truth, especially since they could never go back to the way they were.

By the time Rachel finished outlining the horror of living with Evan, Jillie was outraged. She jumped to her feet, pacing back and forth in front of the fireplace.

"He threatened Mom?" Swearing under her breath, Jillie crossed her arms. "So that's why you wouldn't talk to me alone the last time I was out here."

Rachel couldn't look at Dom. This was the most she'd revealed to him about marriage, and she almost couldn't bear to see his reaction.

"He threatened you, too," Rachel said softly.

Jillie cursed again. "You must have been worried sick. If I'd known, I wouldn't have thought twice. Especially now that I have people who watch out for stuff like that. I guess back then I was just getting started."

"I'm sorry—" Rachel began.

"Don't you *dare* apologize for him." Jillie's eyes blazed. "This is not your fault." She went back to Rachel and wrapped her in a hug. "I'm so sorry."

"Me, too." Though really, Rachel felt ashamed. As if she should have been stronger, fought harder.

Finally she looked at Dom, whose expression had become dark as any thundercloud. He pushed himself out of his chair and knelt in front of her. "From now on, you can only go forward. Stop beating yourself up about the past. You only did what anyone would to protect her family."

More grateful than she should have been, Rachel raised her head. For several beats of her heart, she and Dom stared, gazes locked. For one crazy moment, she thought he might kiss her, right there in front of her sister. Worse, for one crazy moment, she thought she might let him.

"Ahem." Jillie cleared her throat. "I'm here, guys. Remember me?"

Rachel felt her face heat. Dom, on the other hand, gave one of his sardonic smiles.

"You might as well tell me," Jillie continued. "What is really going on between you two?"

"Nothing," Rachel said.

Jillie looked at Dom.

"Really." He laughed. "She hired me to prove she didn't kill her husband. Nothing more."

Jillie's mouth fell open. "Seriously?" When Rachel nodded, she shook her head. "You've got guts, lady. I'll give you that. I would have been scared to even contact him again."

"Not guts, desperation." Feeling suddenly weary, Rachel dragged her hand through her hair. "The authorities really, truly think I killed him. They're working double-time trying to prove it."

"Can you blame them?" Jillie exchanged a glance with Dom. "Anyone would have killed the SOB."

Rachel decided to let that go. "And now someone wants to hurt my baby. Evan had some sort of list of names, people who were involved in various business deals with him. If I don't hand this list over, this man is threatening Cole."

Though she'd touched on all of this briefly in the phone conversation with her sister, Rachel hadn't gone into much detail. Finally, though, she told the worst of it, the part she hadn't even been able to bring herself to tell Dom. "Worse, they're trying to make it look like I'm a danger to my son, that I might hurt him for his inheritance. The police insinuated as much, claiming they'd received a tip."

"So if he dies, you get it all?"

"Not according to the terms of the will and the prenup I signed." She shrugged. "Sure, I could get an attorney and fight, and most likely win. But the settlement I am to receive is quite generous, especially considering the way Evan and I loathed each other."

Dom swore. "I'd like to see a copy of the will."

Rachel looked from Jillie to Dom and then down at her hands. "I don't have one. His attorney hasn't given me anything yet. It's still in probate."

Dom looked grim. "I need his name and address. You and I will need to make a trip over there to talk to him. Do the police know about this?"

"Yes, and the FBI, too. They didn't seem to think it was all that significant. Of course, they're hell-bent on believing I'm the evil villain."

If Dom was going to see the will, he'd learn about Evan's final jab, the provision forbidding her from having any kind of relationship until Cole turned eighteen. She sighed. Maybe that would be for the best. Maybe then Dom would know better than to act on any residual feelings he might have for her.

"I'd really like to freshen up," Jillie said. "Twelve hours in the car has made me feel like a limp noodle."

"Of course." Rachel dug out a card key. "I've got a room all ready right next door."

"Fantastic! I crave a hot shower and a short nap." Jillie jumped up, grinning. "Lead the way."

After hugging her sister and promising to send a wake up call in three hours, Rachel returned to her suite. Dom waited, still sprawled out in her favorite leather chair, looking right at home in the massive furniture.

"Come here, Rach." He patted the side of the chair.

Ignoring him, she chose to sit on the couch instead. "You know, in all the excitement, I didn't sleep too well last night. A nap is sounding pretty good to me, too."

If he got the hint, he chose to ignore it. Instead, he uncoiled himself from his chair and moved to drop down next to her.

She refused to feel overwhelmed at his nearness, despite the way she could feel her suddenly rapid pulse in the hollow of her throat. Dom had once loved to place his lips there and…

Stop it! Giving herself a mental shake, she regarded him with what she hoped was a serene expression.

Gaze smoldering, he twined a lock of her hair around his finger. "Why didn't you leave him, Rachel? You could have come back to me. I would have moved heaven and earth to stop that bastard."

"Right." The old bitterness crept back into her voice. "Dom, I broke our engagement. Even if I'd been able to leave him, I would never think I had the right to come back to you. Not then and—" she paused for emphasis "—not now. Plus, he is—was—a powerful man, Dom. Not only would he have hurt Jillie and Mom, he would have hurt you, too. He made that clear in no uncertain terms."

Dom swore. "All this time, I thought you were happy." When he spoke again, he sounded raspy. "I wish I'd known."

Instead of answering, she looked away.

"Rachel, look at me." He cupped her chin.

Reluctantly, she let him turn her face to his. He was going to kiss her. She knew from the way his breathing had changed, becoming fast and shallow, from how his eyes darkened, telling her without words what her body already knew.

A primal shudder of raw wanting went through her. He was going to kiss her and, as much as she wanted him to, she had to tell him no. She could never sacrifice her son's inheritance for her own desires. She had to refuse. Cole's entire future was at stake.

"Dom, wait." She pushed him away. "There's something I have to tell you. Something about Evan's will."

"It can wait," he growled, and slanted his mouth over hers.

Kissing Rachel was a mistake. But he'd never wanted something so badly. Covering her mouth with his, he meant to merely sample, one chaste taste for old time's sake, but like a starving man given a banquet, he couldn't stop.

Instead, he deepened the kiss, drinking her in, tongues mating. Drowning, drowning.

She made a soft cry that, while fanning the fire of his already inflamed body, made him realize the depths of his mistake.

With an oath, he pulled away, his breathing harsh, hers equally so.

Eyes wide, Rachel stared up at him, looking stunned and so damned beautiful he nearly gave in to the temptation to kiss her again.

Instead, he jackknifed up off the coach. "I won't apologize." With a look, he dared her to demand one.

"Then I will," she said, her voice shaky. "I'm—"

"Don't you dare." He took a deep breath, willing himself to project a calm he didn't feel. "Kissing you was just like old times. Better."

Her brows rose. "You have a good memory."

With a shrug, he discounted her words. "It's only been seven years."

"Seven years is a long time."

Not really, but if she didn't realize that, he wouldn't try to convince her otherwise. He smiled instead.

"Kissing you, making love to you, is something I would never forget, even if it had been a hundred years. Are you telling me you have?"

She looked away. "I've made p-p-p-peace with the p-p-past."

While he never had, or so she was implying. But Rachel was lying. He pretended not to remember what her stutter meant. "Good for you."

"I guess." Biting her lip, she looked down at her hands.

For a moment, he studied her, his beautiful liar. No, not *his*—if he let himself think that, *he* would be the liar. He forced his legs to carry him to the door, though the strength of his erection made walking painful. "I'm going to go talk to some more employees. Let me know when you're ready to return to your house."

"Dom, wait. I still need to tell you about Evan's will."

Shaking his head, he waved her away. "Tell me later. I've got to go." He took off—hobbled, really—without waiting to hear anything more.

Once around the corner, he stopped and leaned against the wall. No way was he talking to anyone, not until he got his body back under control.

Instead, he headed off for the spa and a bracing cold shower.

Once Dom left, Rachel was too wired to nap. Since she couldn't leave Cole alone, she paced the suite, wondering how it could be that Dom's kiss could still affect her with the force of an F5 tornado.

God help her, the man still wanted her. Even after all she'd put him through. If she let him get too close, she'd end up hurting him again.

She had to tell him about the will. She needed to say she had no room in her life for anyone but her son. God help her, she'd tried, but he wouldn't let her. Still, she'd try again. Before either of them did something even more foolish than kiss.

An hour later, Cole padded sleepily into the living area. "Mommy? I'm hungry."

"Let's get you something to eat." As she reached for the phone to call room service, it began to ring. She paused, afraid it might be the threatening caller, then picked it up.

"I'm starving!" Jillie's energetic voice announced. "Can I come over so we can get something to eat?"

"Sure. Cole and I were going to get room service. Come join us."

Jillie laughed. "We still think alike. I'll be right there."

Five minutes later, Jillie arrived. And when Rachel opened the door for her, Dom stood behind Jillie, his expressionless face revealing nothing of what had happened earlier.

Rachel told herself she was glad. The more impersonally they could act toward each other, the better.

They ordered a sample of everything: hamburgers and steak, chicken tacos, salad, soup, fruit, five kinds of dessert. Since Rachel was the boss, her staff made her order top priority and the food arrived in a little over twenty minutes.

Jillie kept up a steady stream of chatter while they pigged out, directing most of her conversation toward Cole. At first uncertain, he finally relaxed enough to joke back.

"We made a sizeable dent on that mountain of food." Jillie leaned back, patting her perfectly flat stomach. "I'm stuffed."

"Me, too," Cole announced, reaching for the last bit of chocolate-syrup-drenched brownie. "This was fun."

"Rach?" Jillie gave her a message-laden look. Rachel knew, without her sister saying another word, what she meant.

"Cole? How would you like to go on a vacation with your Aunt Jillie?"

Cole blinked. "Where? Disneyland?"

He sounded so hopeful they all laughed.

"No, Colorado. Your aunt has a really awesome house up in the mountains and you guys are going to drive there together."

"Oh." He didn't appear too impressed. "Do they have dinosaurs?"

"No," Jillie piped in. "But we have miniature golf and a cool water slide up in Estes Park."

"I guess that'd be okay." Disinterested, he wandered off in search of his toy cars.

"We need to pack," Rachel called after him. "Your aunt wants to leave tomorrow morning."

Engrossed in making two cars crash, he didn't answer.

"Are you going to have a driver go with you?" Dom leaned forward, giving Rachel a long look before turning his attention to Jillie. "I thought all you famous types did. In fact, where's your bodyguard?"

She grinned ruefully. "Normally, I have an entourage. But this is family business. I wanted to handle this by myself, incognito."

"Still, it's a long drive from here to Denver."

"Piece of cake." Jillie waved off his concern. "I'll be rested. Plus, if I get tired, I won't try to make the entire twelve hours in one straight shot. I'll drive until I need to stop, then I'll find a hotel."

"Why don't you stay a couple of days?" Eyes on Cole, Rachel knew Jillie would understand she didn't want to part from her son just yet. "You haven't even visited the house."

"*His* house, you mean. I have no desire to go there. I'll pass. I want to stay the night here." Jillie glanced at Dom. "And we need to leave in the morning."

"But—"

"Rachel." Both Jillie and Dom spoke at once. "It's not safe for him here. Your two days runs out tomorrow afternoon."

They were right, but that didn't mean she had to like it.

"Fine." Rachel nodded. "Morning it is."

For the rest of the evening, they chattered about all the details they'd missed in each other's lives. Finally, they parted ways, each heading off to their separate rooms to sleep. She'd given Dom a room at the far end of the hall.

The next morning, they met again for a room service breakfast in Rachel's suite. Dom seemed preoccupied, making Rachel wonder if he'd managed to learn something while questioning her employees the previous night. She made a mental note to question him after Jillie and Cole were gone.

Watching her sister wave off the bellman and load the luggage into her trunk herself, Rachel gripped Cole's hand with an ache in her throat.

She'd never been separated from her son. When Dom put his hand on her shoulder, she almost lost it. Only knowing she had to be calm and strong for Cole's sake kept her from blubbering like a baby.

"Mommy?" Cole's lower lip trembled. "I want you to come with us, too."

"I wish I was going." Crouching down to put her face on a level with his, she rubbed noses. "But the Batmobile only has room for two people with all that luggage."

"There's two seats in the back." He pointed. "Aunt Jillie said I have to sit in one. You can sit in the other one." Squinting at her, he sighed. "Or even in the front seat, so long as you come with us."

"You know, that's not a bad idea." She pretended to consider it. "Except I've got to keep the hotel running, so I can't leave right now. But I want you to have fun with your aunt Jillie."

Sniffling, he swiped at his eyes with the back of his hand. "But—"

"You're a big boy now." Rachel stood, afraid he'd notice she, too, blinked back tears. "You'll have a great vacation in Denver. There are mountains and lots of stuff to do."

"But I'll miss you," he wailed.

Her heart, already patched together, cracked a little more. "I'll miss you, too. But we'll talk on the phone every day."

"Promise?"

She crossed her heart. "Promise."

"Are you coming, squirt?" In her designer clothes, with one hip cocked and one hand on the ridiculously expensive car door, Jillie looked every bit the famous country singer.

"Okay." Reluctantly, Cole shuffled forward. Halfway there, he stopped and snuck a glance at Dom. "What about him?" He pointed, a hint of desperation in his voice. "Maybe he could come with me?"

Dom played along. "How about it, boss?" he asked Rachel, grinning ear to ear. "Can I go on vacation too?"

Briefly, she actually considered it. Cole needed a body-guard, but if Dom left, she'd have no one here to help prove her innocence. "Well—" she started.

"I have my own people," Jillie interrupted, a tinge of warm understanding coloring her voice. "They guard me, and they'll guard him. Come on, squirt. Let's get this show on the road."

Once Cole had been buckled into his car seat in the back seat, Rachel and Jillie hugged. "Be careful." Rachel knew her twin could see the major effort she was making not to break down in front of her son.

"I will."

Dom hung back.

"Come here, you." Jillie squeezed him in a quick hug. "Take care of her, you hear me?"

"I will," Dom promised solemnly. "Believe me, I will."

The Bentley started with a refined rumble. With a wave, Jillie pulled out. The last glimpse Rachel had of her son was Cole, looking lost and forlorn, waving.

Chapter 7

As soon as Jillie's expensive car disappeared from view, Dom turned to go back inside. Instead, he caught Rachel with an expression of such misery, he couldn't help but pull her into his arms.

"Everything's going to be all right," he murmured, inhaling the herbal-shampoo scent of her hair.

She stiffened, pushing him away. "I sure wish I shared your optimism." She stalked off.

As she crossed the lobby, instead of heading toward her private elevator, she turned in the direction of her office. He followed silently, aware she needed to sort through her emotions.

Once they reached her office, she pushed open the door and sank into her plush chair. Resting her elbows on the polished desk, she chose to focus on business. "What am I going to do, Dom? My time is running out and we're no closer than before to finding the list. What if Evan destroyed it?"

Cautiously, he remained standing. "The Feds have been here longer," he pointed out. "They must not have found anything, either, or they would have already nailed you."

"There's nothing to find." She sounded so weary, he ached to hold her again.

Instead, he kept his feet firmly planted exactly where he stood. "Tell me about Evan's will."

Her inky lashes flew up. "Why now?"

"The police report noted the will had been sealed. I'm guessing they're working on a court order to unseal it. Once they do that, it will become public. What did Evan do that requires such secrecy?"

"I already told you, Evan's attorney hasn't even revealed everything to *me*. He only told me two things that Evan wanted me to know. I've called him a couple of times trying to see a copy. The man won't return my calls."

"What two things?" Dom took a step towards her. "That Cole inherits everything?"

"Yes."

When she didn't elaborate, he dropped into one of the chairs in front of her desk. "And?" he prompted. "What was the other?"

She lifted her chin. "Evan stipulated I'm not to have another relationship until Cole turns eighteen, or Cole loses everything."

Disbelieving, he stared. "Is that legal?"

"Evidently. Otherwise, how could his attorney have written it into the will?"

"You need to hire your own lawyer and fight this."

"Evan's lawyer says that's another stipulation. If I contest the will, Cole loses everything."

Dom swore. "Nevada's a community property state."

"I signed a prenup." Meeting his gaze without flinching, she continued. "Evan orchestrated everything. He left nothing to chance."

Dom wanted to punch the wall. How could Rachel, fiery, independent Rachel, have changed so much that she meekly accepted all this? Her resigned tone had him gritting his teeth.

"Can we please talk about something else now?" She lifted her chin. "Like finding the list."

"Fine. The damn list. If Evan left nothing to chance, there's a possibility he might have destroyed it."

"He didn't know he was going to die. Evan preferred convenience. I think he hid it somewhere so obvious everyone overlooks it, whether at the house or here at the hotel. Whoever killed Evan was probably one of the names on that list. I imagine when they didn't find it when they killed him, they tore the place apart looking."

He started at that. "Tore the place apart? Nothing was mentioned in the police report about that."

"I know. Whoever killed Evan was careful. I only know they searched because certain personal belongings were out of place." She sighed. "Evan was very meticulous and organized. Everything had to be just so, exactly. He was obsessive-compulsive. A paperweight turned the wrong way on his desk was a major upset to him."

"You didn't tell the police about that, did you? It wasn't noted in the report."

"No." Massaging her temples with her fingers, she gave a huge sigh. "We've got to find it, Dom. It's here somewhere or the killer wouldn't be calling me demanding I hand it over."

"We will." He spoke with a confidence he only partially felt.

"At least I can devote more time to searching now that I don't have to worry about Cole." With a grimace, she glanced around the room. "I miss him, Dom. He's too young to be without his mother."

"It won't be for long."

"Hopefully. But if I go to prison, Jillie will have to raise him." She made this pronouncement in a voice so bleak, a chill ran down his spine. "Even if he gets to visit me occasionally, he won't remember me by the time I get out— *if* I get out."

"Don't talk like that." Pushing up out of his chair, he moved around the desk until he stood behind her, and placed his hands on her slender shoulders. He began massaging, remembering how she'd always loved this, claiming it helped release her tension. Though he knew he had no right, knew, too, she might stop him, he couldn't seem to help himself.

"You'll be fine," he told her, his voice husky, his head swimming from the smooth feel of her soft skin.

Holding herself rigid, she refused to relax into his touch. Yet this time, she didn't push him away. "You don't understand, Dom. You don't know what it's like to have a child."

Her comment struck deep. Though he knew she hadn't meant her words to hurt him, they did. He stepped back, trying to find the words to tell her how he felt.

When she looked at him, he shook his head. "That's where you're wrong, Rachel. I do understand. I might never have had a child, but I wanted one. Or two. Ours. Your leaving took that possibility away from me. And I know about hitting rock bottom, something I hope you never have to experience. You might think you're there, but you're not. Not by a long shot."

For a moment his throat clogged and he couldn't go on. Then, he met her gaze and found the strength to continue. "To this day I've never spoken about this. Not to my brother, my sister, not to anyone. My personal lowest was when I realized I could either blow my brains out or pull myself out of the dark hole my life had become and try to start over. At least I had that option. Raymond, my partner, did not."

As she was about to speak, her cell rang. He gestured for her to answer it, needing the interruption. From her side of the conversation, he could tell that Jillie and Cole were checking in. Rachel's next words caught his attention. "Oh, my God. Are you both all right?"

Dom reached for her, freezing when she waved him back, still holding the phone with a white-knuckled grip. "How far away are you? Dom and I will come get you."

Jillie must have argued, because Rachel pursed her lips in the way she did when she didn't like what she was hearing.

"Did you call the police? Good, good. And the other guy, did they catch him? No? What do you mean you're continuing on? What if he comes after you again? What about Cole? How can you make sure he's okay if—"

Her tone changed from frantic to soothing. "Hi, baby. Oh, yeah? Is she? I'm betting that car of hers *does* go fast.

And off-road too, just like Dom? Wow! Maybe you should come—" Rachel bit her lip, evidently having been cut off mid-sentence. "Jillie, you didn't even let me say bye to him. Yes, I know you have *people*. But how quickly can they get there? All right, all right. Call me when you know anything else."

Closing her phone with a snap, she stared at Dom, her expression dazed. "Someone evidently followed them. He slammed into Jillie's car from behind, trying to get her to stop. When she wouldn't, he chased after her, then turned down some shortcut and ended up in front of her." Her slender throat worked.

Dom clenched his hands into fists. One thing he did know for certain—Rachel wasn't trying to kill her son.

"Jillie said this guy slammed on his brakes. She swerved so she wouldn't hit him and ended up next to him. Then he rammed into the side of her car, more than once. Finally, he knocked her off the road."

"Did they roll the car?"

"No, thank God."

"They're okay?"

"Yes." Rachel took a huge, shuddering breath. "Jillie says she got out and pointed her pistol at him and he took off."

"Jillie packs a pistol?" He was surprised. And impressed.

"Yes." Rachel gave him a trembling, but genuine smile. "She said she believes in being prepared."

"Did she get a good look at the guy?"

"She said no." She groaned. "I can't believe this is happening. I don't understand why. My time isn't up yet."

"He must be here, inside the casino. He saw you were

sending Cole away, out of his reach." Frustrated, Dom paced. "There must be a way to catch him."

She shook her head. "I'd rather concentrate on finding the damn list. Then Cole could come home."

"She's not bringing him back, is she?"

"No. She's continuing on." Gaze worried, voice troubled, Rachel stood and jammed her hands into her pockets. "I think she should come back. I didn't know this lunatic would go after her. Cole would be much safer with me. With us."

He ignored the small part of him that foolishly warmed at the *us* and concentrated on convincing her. "Rach, you know Jillie's right. A big country music star like her must have tons of security. To protect her from crazed fans and all that. It's much better to get Cole away from here, especially once we find that list. Jillie can protect him. She even packs a pistol. I had no idea your twin was such a self-sufficient woman. She's grown up a lot since I last saw her."

"We've all grown up." Passing her hand across her eyes, she shuddered. "But Cole is my baby. If anything happens to him…"

"Nothing will," he swore. "This guy wants the list. He doesn't really want to hurt your son, just to use him as leverage against you."

"But then what? What's he going to do with this list once he has it?"

He shrugged. "I'm thinking he plans to use it to blackmail someone."

"You don't think he's one of the names Evan listed?"

"No. If that were the case, every guy who'd ever interacted with Evan would be lurking around here. I'm thinking most of them don't know or don't believe the list even exists. After all, what reason would a man like Evan have for keeping one? He'd only be indicting himself along with the others."

One of the front desk clerks tapped on the partially opened door. After conferring with her for a moment, Rachel turned to Dom. "I'm sorry. I've got to go welcome a major player at the front desk. Feel free to look around wherever. I'll get back with you as soon as I'm finished."

After she left, Dom did a quick search of her office, finding nothing. Dropping into the chair she'd recently vacated, he leaned back, put his feet up on her desk and tried to think of a better plan of action.

They were running out of time. Maybe he should call in the big guns.

Like his brother.

Dom needed Sebastian's help now. Not only to keep Cole safe, but if Nathan had told the truth and the Feds were getting near trying for an indictment on Rachel, time was running out. He had to find the list. As far as he could tell, the elusive list was the only thing that would make anyone even consider the possibility that someone besides Rachel had killed her former husband.

With his emotionless, practical approach to everything, Sebastian might have more success. Taking out his phone, Dom punched the number up on speed dial.

"Hello?" Seb answered on the second ring. "Dom, what's up? How's it going out there in Vegas?"

"Hey again." Dom overlooked the lack of emotion in Seb's tight voice. He couldn't help the way he'd become. "How's Gramps doing?"

Seb sighed. "The doctors say it could be any time. But they haven't told us to start gathering in the family, so I'm guessing we've got at least a couple of weeks. Phillip's too ornery to die. When are you coming home?"

"I'm not." Chest tight, Dom cleared his throat. "I need you to come to Vegas."

"Are you all right?" Though Seb's tone still sounded remote and unconcerned, Dom knew the Cordasic family code would ensure Seb would help. Loyalty was in their genes. "You haven't started hitting the bottle again, have you?"

"Of course not. I'm working on a case and I need your help." He filled his brother in on the situation with Rachel, her murdered husband and the elusive list.

Sebastian went silent when Dom wound down. Finally, he cleared his throat. "This doesn't sound good. Are you sure you really want to do this, man? Have you seriously thought this through?"

Knowing his brother saw right through him. Dom closed his eyes for a second. "Of course I want to help Rachel. She's innocent. She doesn't deserve to go to jail."

"Is she really, Dom? Innocent? Are you thinking with your head or with another part of your anatomy?"

Gritting his teeth, Dom bit back a sharp retort. "This has nothing to do with our previous relationship. It's professional. She hired me to find this list and prove she didn't kill her husband."

"Uh-huh." Seb didn't believe him. Worse, Dom couldn't blame him. He didn't even believe himself. He could picture Sebastian, kicked back in a chair, with his feet crossed at the ankles, shaking his head in disbelief.

"Dom, do you really think Rachel is telling the truth?"

"Yes."

"You're really vulnerable right now, Dom." Seb warned. "You haven't even been sober two years yet."

"Eighteen months." This was one topic Dom didn't want to discuss. His resistance to the beer earlier had proved his strength to himself.

"What happens if you and Rachel get involved again?"

"She can't." Briefly, he told his brother about Evan's will.

"Wow." Seb whistled. "But you're forgetting I know you, bro. Have you told her about your inheritance?"

"What inheritance? Phillip disowned me, remember?"

"Yeah, but—"

"Come on, Seb," Dom interrupted. "There's no need to rub my face in all the things I've given up. Yeah, I'd love to have the money, but you and I both know I want to redeem myself in Phillip's eyes more. I'm asking for your help."

"Which you never did in the past, even though I would have given anything to help you. But this…I don't know…. You really loved her, man."

"I know." Dom dragged his hand across his jaw. "You don't have to tell me that."

"Are you completely over her?"

Dom saw no reason to lie. "No."

"That's what I was afraid of. This has got to be killing you."

"No. I'm doing all right. I think."

"Are you?" Seb sounded as if he didn't believe him. "Let me check flight info. I'll be there as soon as I can."

After he hung up, Dom smiled. If anyone could help furrow out the truth, Sebastian could.

Though she'd already searched every square inch of the hotel, Rachel checked again. It didn't help that the Lone

Star had over fifty computers and Evan could have stashed his precious list in any of them. Not to mention all the portable storage options, from old-fashioned, floppy diskettes to CDs and memory sticks. Assuming her former husband had decided to go with modern technology.

Knowing Evan, she suspected he had not. The information had probably been handwritten in one of those leatherbound journals in which he'd been so fond of writing.

Still, since all the computers were networked, she'd checked them first, then she'd gone to each workstation and collected every CD or floppy diskette she could find. She'd taken them all to her office and reviewed the contents of each and every one.

No list.

She covered her face with her hands, refusing to cry, and tried to think. Evan had laughed at the threats. Where would he have hidden something so important? She couldn't shake the feeling she was missing something. Some painfully obvious clue dangling right in front of her, if she could only open her eyes and see it.

Sebastian arrived unannounced the next day, either forgetting to call ahead or choosing not to. He phoned Dom's room from the front desk at 7:00 a.m., just as Dom finished drying off from his shower.

"I'm here." Two terse words, nothing more.

"Come on up. I'm in room—"

"No. You come down. I'll wait for you in the Panhandle Café." Sebastian hung up without waiting for an answer.

Hurriedly, Dom brushed his teeth and got dressed. Even at this hour, he suspected there'd be long lines at the café, since a convention of party-happy orthopedic surgeons had arrived the previous afternoon.

He and Rachel had expected to hear from the caller once the deadline passed, but no word had come. Edgy and irritable, they'd gone their separate ways late last night. He hoped she'd gotten more rest than he had.

When he arrived at the café entrance, his brother was nowhere in sight.

One of the helpful hostesses pointed him in the right direction. "Ms. Adair took him to the lounge."

Of course. No matter the hour, Sebastian always made it a priority to have a drink first thing after a flight. If he could imbibe with a beautiful woman at his elbow, so much the better.

The hotel lounge was empty at this time of the day. Dom located Rachel and his brother quickly, pausing near the entrance to watch them unobserved. For a man who'd been so unenthusiastic about learning Rachel was back in Dom's life, Sebastian sure didn't show it. Elbows on the table, he eyed her with rapt attention while she talked.

Though Dom couldn't blame him, he hated the instant flare of jealousy inside. He had no right to be jealous. If his brother wanted to flirt with Rachel, fine with him.

As Dom walked across the room, Rachel placed her hand on Seb's arm, smiling as she spoke. Seb bent close and replied. Whatever he'd said made Rachel toss her blond hair back and laugh, looking so beautiful she made Dom's throat tight.

"Hey, you two." Fixing a smile on his face, Dom waved. "I see you found Rachel."

"No, she found me." Seb jumped up and gave him a bear hug. "She recognized me standing in that horrible line."

Rachel grinned up at him. "Why didn't you tell me your brother was coming?"

"Because he promised to call me with flight info and he didn't."

Seb shook his head. "I didn't have time for details. You said you needed me. Here I am."

"And I'm glad to see you, bro. It's been way too long." Dom slid in the booth next to Rachel. "I supposed Rachel filled you in."

"She did." Sebastian took a long swig of his Bloody Mary. "And she ordered me breakfast."

"How about you?" she asked, still smiling. "Would you like something to eat? I'm having the café bring it over here."

"Sure." He ordered an omelet and coffee, staring at his brother. "You look the same."

"So do you." Sebastian gave his version of a smile. "Man, I have to tell you, Phillip wasn't happy when I told him where I was going."

"I'm not surprised."

"But he did say something encouraging," Seb continued. "He asked me to let him know if you were still off the sauce and how your business is going."

"That's encouraging."

"Yeah." Their breakfast arrived and they spent the next several minutes digging in.

Once Seb polished off his eggs, bacon and toast, he leaned back in his chair and sipped his Bloody Mary. "Before I came out here, I did some research of my own on Evan Adair. No wonder the FBI is investigating. The man had his hands in just about every conceivable illegal activity. Allegedly." He held up his hand. "Though no one's been able to pin anything on him. Yet. But if this mythical list really exists…"

Dom exchanged a look with Rachel. "I told him about the list."

Rachel looked at Sebastian. "What do you think?"

"Word on the street is that everybody and his brother is looking for that list."

"Then why won't the police believe me? They keep acting like I'm making everything up." Rachel sighed. "The Las Vegas Metro acted like I was crazy and the FBI flat-out told me I was imagining things."

"Interesting. The Feds never ignore stuff like that. Someone is lying to you. They just want you to *think* they don't believe you." Seb rattled the ice in his glass. "Or maybe someone's setting you up."

"Of course." Rachel grimaced. "I've been saying that all along. Whoever it is has the ear of the police, that's for sure." Eyes shining, she sat up straight. "When I prove the list exists, the police will have other suspects for Evan's murder."

"That can be a dangerous thing, too," Sebastian commented. "If someone was willing to kill once to keep their name from going public…"

"They'd be willing to kill again," Dom finished for him.

"Do you really think that's why Evan was killed? Because of his precious list?" She looked from one man to the other.

"Most likely." Draining his drink, Seb put the empty glass on the table. "Either he was using it to blackmail someone or one of the heavy hitters realized how much such a list could implicate him."

"But just because someone's name is on a list doesn't prove anything. There'd have to be proof."

"I'm sure there's backup on everything. Details of the operations, all that sort of thing" Dom signaled the bartender. When the man walked over, he pointed to Seb's glass. "Do you want another?"

"No. One's my limit." Seb ordered a diet cola. "Someone as meticulous as Evan wouldn't leave anything to chance."

"Or Nathan." Dom shook his head. "That SOB always did look out for numero uno."

"Nathan?"

"Frederick. He's SAC."

"Damn," Seb said. "That little prick just won't go away, will he?"

Back when Dom had worked for the Bureau and Seb for the military, Seb had met Nathan during a hostage situation involving a high-ranking military officer's daughter.

"No, he won't." Dom drank the last of his coffee. "I spoke to him when I first got in. He told me everything Rachel said was a lie."

Rachel touched the back of Dom's hand. "See what I mean? It's like there's some sort of giant conspiracy against me."

Any reply Dom might have made stuck in his throat. He couldn't look away from Rachel. He thought he could drown in her amazing blue eyes. The tiny dimple that always appeared in her cheek so captivated him, he forgot about his brother, forgot the bar, the will, even forgot what they'd been talking about.

He wanted to kiss her. Hell, he wanted to do much more than that, but a kiss would do for now.

He actually started leaning in to do exactly that, when the sound of Sebastian clearing his throat stopped him.

Both he and Rachel turned to look at Sebastian. "What?" Dom knew he sounded gruff.

"We need to talk. Alone." Sliding off the bar stool, Sebastian grabbed his arm. "Will you excuse us?" he asked Rachel.

Expression slightly dazed, she nodded.

"We'll see you later, then."

Sebastian steered Dom out into the hall and into the nearest men's restroom. Luckily, the place was deserted.

"What the hell is wrong with you?" Seb's attempt at anger was pretty damn convincing. Despite being unable to experience emotions, Sebastian knew how he was supposed to feel and tried to act the part.

"I—"

"Damn it, Dom. You're getting emotionally involved with her again."

"Not going to happen," Dom scoffed. "You're forgetting about the will."

"You don't give a rat's ass about the will. Good lord, man. I saw the cow eyes you two were making at each other. You were about to kiss her."

"No, I wasn't." Dom crossed his arms.

The disgusted look on Sebastian's face showed what he thought of that. "You've never been able to lie to me, bro. Don't start now."

Exhaling, Dom shook his head. "Sorry. Being around Rachel is a problem. Whatever we once had, I think it's still there."

"Are you sure it's not one-sided? After all, the woman needs your help. Once she gets what she wants, she'll do the same thing she did before."

They both knew what that was. Break Dom's heart.

"I won't let her," Dom said, wishing he felt as convinced as he sounded.

"Good." Seb let him go. "Because you'd really be screwing up. I didn't want to tell you in front of Rachel, but there's a chance Phillip will agree to see you."

Dom stared. "Are you serious?"

"Yes. You know how he likes to control everything. The other thing he asked me to check on was Rachel. He never forgave her for what she did to you, you know. He saw her on the news when they ran that story about Evan's death. He said he might want you to come see him before the end, provided you aren't involved with her."

Chapter 8

Watching Dom and his brother leave, Rachel kept her chin up until they'd disappeared from view. Then and only then did she let her rigid spine sag.

Stupid, stupid, stupid.

She'd almost kissed Dom again. Right in front of his brother and anyone else who might have happened to walk into the bar, in the casino her husband had owned. All she needed was for some news-hungry journalist to start hinting she'd been having an affair before her husband's death. One more reason—even though it wasn't true—for her to have murdered Evan.

The police would have a field day with that one.

And worse, so would Evan's attorney. Cole's inheritance would vanish in the blink of an eye or, in this case, with one touch of the lips.

Damn! She had to get this attraction under control.

Independent, self-sufficient women didn't make these kinds of mistakes. Mothers who wanted to protect their son's inheritance sure as hell didn't.

Leaving the bar, she headed down to the conference room she'd designated for Nathan Frederick and his team. One thing she could do was get to the bottom of this list-or-no-list thing. The existence of the list could save her from being wrongly accused of murder.

Nathan had been lying to her, and she wanted to know why.

Nathan looked up when she entered the conference room. His smile made her skin crawl, though she told herself he was only trying to be pleasant. Forcing herself to smile back, she dropped into the lone chair in front of the table he was using as a desk.

"Rachel, so good to see you." The warmth of his tone didn't match the coldness in his gaze, especially when he looked her over like a farmer buying a cow at market. "I've been too busy to eat breakfast. Would you like to have a bite with me?"

The way he worded his question, along with the blatant invitation in his gaze, nearly made her gag.

Reminding herself to play nice, Rachel swallowed. "I've already eaten," she said. "I really just wanted to talk to you about Evan's list."

He kept his pasted-on shark's smile. "Rachel. You know the list is only a rumor. There is no such thing."

Why did he continue to lie?

Feeling reckless—after all, she had nothing to lose—Rachel leaned forward. If he wanted to play games, she could do the same. "But Agent Frederick, the list does exist. I know, because I've found it."

He froze. For a heartbeat his pleasant expression vanished, revealing raw fury. Then, so quickly she might have imagined it, the other Nathan was back, smiling indulgently.

"Really?" He raised a brow in a manner she suspected was meant to infuriate her. "Let me take a look at it."

"It's in a safe place." She wondered if he could arrest her if she refused to show it to him. Which would be impossible, since she had no idea where the list was actually hidden.

Staring at her with cold, flat eyes, Nathan continued smiling. "Rachel, we're about to ask the D.A. to convene a grand jury. We think we have enough information to ask for an indictment against you."

When she didn't respond, he let his smile fade away. "A murder indictment, Rachel. What will happen to your son if you're taken into custody pending trial?"

A murder indictment? Was he telling the truth? Or was this his way of upping the ante?

She wished she'd been a better poker player.

Blankly, she looked at him, hoping her own expression didn't reflect blind panic. "Why are you telling me this?"

"Because you've found the list. Don't you understand? Even proving the existence of such a thing could potentially exonerate you."

What the hell had she gotten herself into? But since she'd already started digging the hole, she might as well deepen it. "You'll see it at the same time as the rest of the world, on Friday. I've told the police about it, and select members of the media. Dominic's keeping it safe for me— and making copies."

"You idiot." Nathan came up out of his chair, reaching for her as if he meant to throttle her. "How can you not understand how important this is?"

"Oh, I do understand." Scooting back, she nearly knocked her chair over in her haste to get out of his reach. "But I need to take precautions. After the way I've been railroaded with Evan's death, I'm making sure to cover my ass."

"Friday is in two days," he snarled. "A lot can happen in two days. What if someone steals the damn thing? Go get it and bring it to me *now*."

Shocked, she could only stare at him, heart pounding. Though inside she was quaking, she hadn't dealt with Evan Adair for seven years without learning a trick or two.

Standing, she straightened her spine and looked him in the eye. "Are you threatening me, Agent Frederick?"

As she'd known he would, he backed down. Dropping back into his chair, he raked his hand through his thinning hair.

"Of course not," he said, as smooth as if their brief altercation had never happened. "Will you at least let me talk to Dominic? Maybe I can talk some sense into him."

"Dominic works for me." Déjà vu. "You can see the list on Friday, like everyone else."

From his set jaw and furious eyes, he didn't like giving in. Tough. "What time Friday?"

"Two o'clock." As lies did, this one got more and more complicated.

"Fine." He picked up the phone and started dialing, effectively dismissing her.

Though her legs felt rubbery, she managed to stroll from the room with what she hoped was an unconcerned air.

Once she rounded the corner, she had to stop and catch her breath and try to calm her racing heart.

She had a feeling she'd just started something that could have far-reaching consequences. Worse, what was she going to do when Friday rolled around and she couldn't produce the list?

Right now she needed to find Dominic and tell him what she'd done.

Promising to meet Dominic that afternoon, Sebastian took off, saying he had phone calls to make. While he was gone, Dom resumed questioning the employees. In two days of back-to-back interviews, he'd learned little, except that each and every one of the Lone Star employees had disliked Evan Adair.

Several hours later, after numerous sessions revealed nothing, Dom decided to take a break and go annoy Nathan. Maybe Nathan's ego would let something slip.

The area that Rachel had allocated to the FBI was a hive of activity. Nathan's team was packing, getting ready to move out. That could mean only one thing—either they'd gotten what they needed, or they'd found nothing.

He located Nathan loading up boxes. Apparently, he'd made it just in time, as Nathan was closing what appeared to be the last box.

Looking up as Dom approached, Nathan regarded him warily. "What do you want, Cordasic?"

"Looks like you guys are done. I take it you found what you needed?"

"You bastard," Nathan snarled. "Having your big brother do your dirty work for you."

Stunned, Dom stared. "I have no idea what you're talking about."

"Right. Like you don't know Sebastian is friends with Paul Kinney."

Paul was the man who'd fired Dominic. He was also Nathan's boss.

"So?"

"So I'm off the case."

Dom couldn't help it, he laughed.

Nathan's gaze filled with fury. "You tell that girlfriend of yours I don't want to wait until Friday."

Though once again Dom had no idea what the other man meant, this time he refused to give him the satisfaction of knowing so. He merely shrugged as though the statement was of no consequence to him and turned to go.

Behind him, Nathan cursed. "You're so smug, Cordasic. You think you know everything, and you don't know jack. So what if my team and I are leaving? Once the list is made public, this entire operation is going to blow wide open. Rachel said you had it and had made copies. Have you even looked at it yet?"

Rachel'd said what? Careful to let his face show nothing, Dom slowly turned. "What are you implying?"

"Maybe you'll never show anyone the list because it will implicate your girlfriend." His tone dripped venomous sarcasm. "Ever wonder about her husband's death? Ever think maybe you might be next?"

"Are you threatening me?" Hands balled into fists, Dom glared at the shorter man.

"Oh, cut the crap. Like you don't know your little chickee is a murderer. She could kill you just as easily, you know."

"Rachel did not kill Evan Adair."

"And pigs can fly." Nathan spat. "You don't have any intention of letting me see the list, do you? Your brother's here. Your family has connections. You're going to try to use this to your advantage, if Rachel lets you."

Dom stared at the man in disbelief. Had he gone insane? A muscle twitched in Nathan's face and the nostrils in his prominent nose flared. His complexion had gone so red he looked about to explode.

"What the hell is wrong with you?" Dom finally asked.

"You and Rachel," Nathan spat the name. "She came in here to gloat and now you're here to do the same. I was just getting ready to go to the D.A. to try for an indictment. But with this list, my case may go out the window." He gave a bitter laugh. "Or maybe I should say my *former* case, thanks to your brother."

Dom let that one go.

Hefting his boxes, Nathan shot Dom a look of disgust. "Make of it what you want, but until I find evidence to the contrary, I plan to make sure the police don't consider your friend innocent. And tell Sebastian this for me—I might be officially off this investigation, but I've got some vacation time coming. I will dig and dig until I find proof Rachel killed her husband. The widow Adair isn't going to get away with murder, not on my watch."

With that, he stormed out of the room.

The widow Adair? Not on my watch? Evidently Nathan had worse delusions of grandeur than Dom had realized. But at least his words proved the Feds had nothing on Rachel. Neither did the police. No DNA, no confession, nothing other than motive in spades. Unfortunately, sometimes motive was enough to convince the D.A. to call a grand jury.

Which led him to the biggest question. Why had Rachel told Nathan the list had been found?

He hurried off to locate Rachel and find out.

"Dom!" Spotting him from across the lobby, Rachel rushed over, dreading his reaction when she told him what she'd done. "I've been looking for you."

"Same here." He glanced around, and she guessed he was assessing whether they could talk without being overheard.

"My office." She led the way. Once inside, she closed the door. Dom watched her expectantly.

"Crud." Rubbing her temple, she attempted a smile, failing miserably. "I told Nathan we'd found the list."

He shot her a sideways look. "Why?"

"I was tired of him acting like judge and jury. He'd already convicted me. I didn't mean to say it, but once I did, I couldn't back down."

"Now what are you going to do?"

She heaved a sigh, glad he wasn't furious at her. But then Dom had always been a pretty even-tempered man. "I don't know, but we've got to find it quickly. Nathan thinks we're having a press conference on Friday."

Dom smiled. "I went to see him. He was packing. He's been taken off the case."

"What?" She couldn't believe it. "How, why?"

"He said Sebastian phoned his boss. I guess my brother called in a favor."

Rachel dropped into her chair. Her legs felt wobbly, like they'd no longer support her. "Dom, Nathan said he had enough to ask for an indictment. How is that possible? I've done nothing."

"He was planning to use the only thing he has—motive."

She bit her lip. "God knows I have plenty of that. But I *didn't* kill him."

"I know." For the space of a heartbeat, he studied her. Her heart turned over in response, even as she called herself a fool. Despite his closed expression, she sensed his vulnerability was equal to her own.

If so, they were both idiots.

Deliberately shutting out her overcharged awareness of him, she pushed herself out of the chair.

"Come on. Let's go find your brother. I want to thank him for getting the Feds off my back."

Dom nodded. "I'm betting he's hanging out in the casino. He used to love to play poker."

Sebastian saw them coming. He collected his chips and met them halfway across the casino floor. "Thought I'd try my hand at blackjack." He smiled his cold, emotionless smile. "I won $5,000 in just thirty minutes."

"Good for you." Rachel laughed. "I'll have to review the security cameras later so I can watch how you play."

"So you can make sure he's not cheating, you mean." Dom grinned at them both. "Drinks are on you, big bro. Coffee for me, though."

"Sebastian, you've been busy." Rachel slipped one arm through his. "Thank you for getting rid of the FBI."

"You're welcome. But it's just Nathan. They'll send someone else to take his place. Unless…" He peered at her expectantly. "You have some news you want to tell me?"

For a moment she was confused, then she realized he'd already heard she had the list. "You're very well connected, aren't you?" she said, stalling for time.

He glanced at Dom, then back at her. "You two don't have the list, do you?"

"No." Rachel admitted, feeling even more foolish than she had when she'd had to tell Dom. Sebastian's dark expression seemed more intimidating somehow.

He let out his breath loudly. "Bet that's a relief, huh?" he asked Dom.

Dom nodded. "Except Nathan will be telling his superiors, including your friend Paul, that we have it and are planning to hold a press conference."

Seb smiled his empty smile and glanced at his watch. "Guess you two had better get busy finding it then. I'm going to see what I can find out about who's taking over from Frederick." With a wave, he walked away.

Rachel's shoulders sagged. "He's right. Since we've searched the hotel endlessly, maybe we should try the house again."

"I'm game." Dom took her arm. "Let's go."

Several hours later, after another search of the Adair house, they met in the great room.

"Nothing," Rachel said, wishing she could hang on to her earlier optimism. "I'm beginning to wonder if the list really even exists."

Dom gave her a wry smile. "Sure would suck for Evan if someone killed him for something that wasn't real."

"You know, there could be a ton of other reasons someone would want Evan dead. He had a lot of enemies."

"Most powerful people do." Dom crossed to the

window, staring out at the pool. "But few of them get killed because of it. No, your husband either double-crossed someone or blackmailed the wrong person with that list."

Was his use of the words *your husband* deliberate? They were talking to each other with the impersonal attitudes of complete strangers.

Glancing at the security camera, she supposed that was for the best. She wished she didn't feel such a pang of regret. "Are you ready to head back to the hotel?"

"It's nearly dinnertime," Dom said without turning. "Do you want to stop and pick up something along the way?"

"Sure." She matched her tone to his. "We haven't had anything since breakfast. I'm starving."

Once they were on the road, Dom headed for the freeway.

"Fast food? Or would you rather find a place we can go in and sit down, away from cameras?"

She looked at him from under her lashes, considering, glad he'd given her a choice. "I think we'd better go with fast food," she said softly.

From the set of his jaw, she could tell he didn't like the answer, but he accepted it. Exiting the freeway, he took them through the drive-through of a local burger place. Ordering them both bacon burgers with cheese, curly fries and diet sodas, he paid and accepted the bags without comment.

"There's an old mining road on the way that has a great view at night," he said. "We can eat there."

A short drive later, they parked and devoured their food. Rachel ate every last greasy fry. When they'd finished, she leaned back against the seat with contentment, staring out at the twinkling lights of Vegas.

"That was lovely," she sighed.

"So are you." The huskiness in his voice made her body tingle. When she turned to look at him, he kissed her, his lips hard and searching.

"Dom." Not exactly a protest, she sighed against his mouth. Then, as if the lack of security cameras finally freed her, she wrapped her arms around his neck and kissed him back.

Challenging, eager, she traced the outline of his lips with her tongue. He shuddered.

"Rach?"

They both knew the question had to be asked.

She wanted him. More than she'd wanted anything in a seven years. Her body felt awakened, her blood roaring through her veins like a springtime river fed by melting snow.

"It's been so long," she murmured. "Oh, Dom…"

"Too long." Moving slowly, carefully, he cupped her breast through her T-shirt. Her nipple firmed instantly.

"Mmm, I…" Whatever she'd been about to say became a soft moan as he trailed his mouth down her throat. "Oh, Dom."

Climbing over the console, he straddled her. "I want you," he growled against her mouth before claiming her again in a deep, drugging kiss.

"I want you, too."

She could barely breathe, so great was her arousal. And joy.

"Rachel?" Ever the gentleman, Dom pulled back, giving her one last chance before they threw caution and restraint to the wind. "Are you sure?"

Feeling fierce, she smiled. She'd never been more sure of anything in her entire life. Instead of answering with words, she reached up and slanted her lips over his, plundering his mouth, making him shudder with a need that matched hers.

When she finally pulled back, the only sound was his harsh, uneven breathing.

She met his gaze, her heart turning over. "Make love to me, Dom. Make me forget. Make me *remember*."

Needing no second invitation, he reached for her and she laughed the low, throaty sound of a woman about to take what she wanted.

"Rachel. My Rachel," he growled. "I've missed you even more than I realized."

Slowly, her gaze never leaving his, Rachel pulled her shirt over her head. Next, she removed her bra, then shimmied out of her jeans. Only her panties remained. Dom hooked his finger in the elastic and helped slide them off.

Eyes dark, he stared at her in moonlight the color of amber. As he unbuttoned his shirt, she had a wild flash of memory, thinking back to the first time they'd made love. He yanked off his jeans, the force of his arousal making her gasp.

They were silver and gold, flame and ice. Dominic and Rachel.

"Dominic…" She held out her arms.

As they became intertwined, he kissed her again, the tip of him touching her wet center. He entered her with one smooth motion and she cried out. They were perfect fit. She sheathed him, his swollen body right where he belonged.

When he began to move, she forgot to think. And when he reached his release, she was there with him, riding the crest, the moon and the stars swirling down from the sky.

Finally, after he'd collapsed against her, he kissed her one more time. "I've missed you," he said.

Unaccountably, she began to weep, great gasping sobs. The unfamiliar sounds coming from her throat were the sounds of an animal in pain.

He held her while she sobbed, stroking her hair and raining kisses on her temples.

Gradually her tears subsided to a sniffle. Ashamed, she pushed at him. He didn't move.

"I'm sorry," she said, wiping at her face. "I didn't mean for that to happen."

"Do you want to tell me?"

"No." She shook her head. "Yes. I don't know. The last time I did what we just did was the last time I was with you."

He frowned. "But you had Cole. Surely you and Evan…"

"Evan raped me." Lifting her chin, she swallowed. "Over and over again, until I got pregnant. Once he'd accomplished that, he never touched me again."

Tension jerked through Dom's body. She felt his hands fist. He said nothing for a time, and then bit by bit she felt him relax. "He's lucky he's already dead." With a tender gesture, he smoothed the hair away from her face. "How did you survive?"

She sniffed again. "It wasn't…violent. He used his threats to get me to cooperate. But I hated him, Dom. For a time, I wanted to die. If not for the fact that he gave me Cole…"

She let the words trail off, unwilling to admit how close to the edge she'd come. "But I had Cole, and I was happy."

Staring at her, he shook his head. "Rachel, why did you—?"

"Enough." She pushed at him again. "We've got to get dressed. What if someone does drive up here?"

"You weren't worried about that a moment ago. Rachel—"

"I am now." She fumbled with her bra. "Dom, this changes nothing. Don't get the wrong idea."

His laugh sounded like a cry. "This changes everything, Rachel. You'll see." He touched her with reverence, something she hadn't experienced in the seven years since she'd left him.

His craggy face was beautiful. Too beautiful for a man so rough. Behind his arrogance, she saw vulnerability. Behind his cold exterior, she saw the spark of heat.

He might hide it, but he was afraid of her. Afraid of their mutual attraction. Maybe, like her, he feared they would drown each other, each fighting to reach the surface, each pulling the other down. Such heat would never be tame or safe.

The rawness of the desire between them shocked her, unsettled her with its potential to ruin her carefully made plans for herself and her son. Some small, foolish part inside her wanted to believe Dom's romantic nonsense, even though nothing could come of it.

"Nothing changes," she insisted, pulling on her shirt and avoiding his gaze. While they dressed, she felt like they were dancing around each other in the front seat of his truck, making a mockery of the intimate act they'd just shared.

"I don't believe you." He ground the words out. "Once again, you prove you value money over love or happiness."

"The will—"

"Forget the will. What if we have been given a second

chance, Rachel? You and I? In my experience, most people don't get second chances. Can you so easily throw that away for an inheritance?"

Anger blazed through her. "I would do anything for my son. I won't jeopardize what's his by right."

"That is the most…" He shook his head and took a deep breath. She knew he was struggling to keep from saying something he'd regret later. "I understand," he finally said, resignation coloring his angry tone. "You know I could force your hand, but I won't."

Though she knew he understood nothing, she didn't comment. He started the truck and they drove back to the Lone Star in silence. Once there, she retreated to her suite, knowing she was in for a long and sleepless night, with Dominic just down the hall.

She was right. She slept little and woke bleary eyed to a call from Sebastian. "Where are you? Dom and I are already having breakfast."

She glanced at the clock. Seven a.m. Late for her. "My alarm didn't go off. I haven't even showered."

"So? Get up, brush your teeth, wash your face and get dressed. Dom and I have a plan. We'll wait for you."

"Does Dom know you're calling me?"

"No. He's at the buffet, getting more food. Why?"

She sighed. "Never mind. I'll be there in ten minutes."

It took her fifteen. When she arrived at the café, both men had already finished eating. She slid into the booth and ordered coffee and fruit.

"What happened to your waiting?" she asked Sebastian, avoiding looking at Dom.

He grinned. "I was hungry."

Her cell phone rang. Distracted, she answered without even checking the caller ID. A man identifying himself as a Denver police officer asked for her.

Nearly dropping the phone, Rachel reached out blindly and gripped Dom's arm for support. "This is she."

In clipped, brusque tones he told her Jillie had been shot, along with two of her bodyguards. She'd been taken to the hospital by ambulance, though her wounds weren't life-threatening.

The police thought it was a carjacking attempt, but Rachel knew better. Someone had tried to snatch Cole. And had nearly killed her sister.

Chapter 9

"My son. Is—is…is he all right?" She could barely force the words past the panic in her throat. When the policeman assured her Cole was fine, her next question was about her sister.

"Ms. Everhart will be all right. She has a gunshot wound to her right thigh, but it's mostly superficial."

"Where'd you send her?"

The officer rattled off the name, address and phone number of a hospital.

"Wait, wait." Grabbing a napkin, Rachel motioned for a pen. Sebastian handed her one and she wrote furiously. As she finished, a stab of panic hit her. "If my sister's in the hospital, who's watching my son?"

"I believe her people are, ma'am." The officer sounded impatient, eager to get off the phone now. "He's perfectly safe."

Closing her phone, she stared blindly at her hand, still gripping Dom's arm. Raising her eyes to his, she managed to tell him what had happened. "He's shot Jillie."

Dom tried to pull her into his arms. Ever mindful of the security cameras, Rachel resisted, though she let him take her hand. Little by little, warmth crept back into her body, though she couldn't stop shivering. Teeth chattering, she told the two men what had happened. "I need to go get my son."

"You can't leave the state," Sebastian pointed out.

"Why not?" Dom shot back. "She hasn't been charged with any crime."

"They'll make it look like she's a flight risk if she tries to go and you know it."

"Then I'll go." Dom sounded fierce.

"No." Sebastian started to say something else, but Rachel cut him off with a glare.

"I need to make sure Cole's okay." Flipping open her cell, she hit speed-dial for Jillie. After six rings, voice mail picked up.

"Of course it would have been too much to hope for that Cole had her phone," she muttered.

"Try her house. If her people are watching him, they most likely took him there."

Still watching, Sebastian crossed his arms and said nothing.

Again, no one answered. Frantic, Rachel blinked back tears. "Why won't someone *talk* to me?"

Next, she tried the hospital. A nurse informed her that Jillie was in surgery and asked if she'd like to leave a message. She left her name and number, her stomach roiling.

"Now what do I do? I can't talk to Jillie, her people won't answer the phone. I've got to make sure Cole is all right."

Sebastian uncoiled himself from his chair. "Give me the address and phone number. I'm leaving in ten minutes."

"I'm going with you," Rachel said, daring him to argue.

"No, you're not." Sebastian strode from the room, calling over his shoulder. "Dom, tell her she has to stay here."

"He's right, you know."

"Cole doesn't even know him!" She stared at Dom, trying not to get hysterical. "He's never met Sebastian. I've taught him stranger danger. He won't go with your brother. You'd better go instead."

Dom shook his head. "By the time Seb gets a flight, you'll have talked to Cole."

"You don't know that. If I can't get through—"

"You'll get through," he soothed. "Cole's safe. Jillie's safe. Don't sweat the small stuff."

"But Jillie's people won't let Seb anywhere near him. They're used to overzealous fans."

"Sebastian knows people. Believe me, he'll get to Cole. I'm sure he'll check in with Jillie at the hospital."

She took a deep breath.

"If anyone can protect Cole, Sebastian can." Dom continued. "You remember what he used to do."

"Special Forces isn't going to help with this. I really think you should go." Rachel swallowed. "I trust you, Dom."

"You need him more than your son does." Sebastian's even-toned voice behind her made her jump. "Do you have the directions?"

"I thought you said ten minutes." Dom smiled grimly.

"Sorry, I was wrong." Sebastian's matching smile was

equally bleak. "I only needed three." He held out his hand. "Give me the hospital information, please."

Reluctantly, Rachel scribbled Jillie's info on a second napkin. "If they won't let you talk to Jillie, I'm going to have to talk to someone first. If Jillie's people have been told to protect Cole, you won't be able to get near him."

"I'll get near him," Sebastian said. "It's what I do for a living." And he was gone.

That night, too nervous to sleep, Rachel took to prowling the hotel. She made two tours of the casino floor before she bumped into Dom. He took one look at her expression and grabbed her arm.

"Come with me. If I ever saw anyone who needed a drink…"

Without asking what she wanted, he ordered her a gin and tonic, telling the bartender to make it a double. He ordered himself a diet cola.

"I prefer wine," she said stiffly, accepting the drink nonetheless. When Dom indicated a chair, she shook her head. "I'm sorry. I can't sit. Not until I know Cole and my sister are safe."

"I understand. Get your drink." Grabbing his own, they walked out of the bar and down the long hallway that lead to the registration area. The noise and smoke faded as they put the casino floor behind them.

"I'm tired of this," she said. "We've got to find the damn list. I want whoever this is to leave Cole alone."

Halfway between reservations and the coffee shop, he stopped, staring down at her. "I agree. It's especially difficult because we don't know whether he put it on a CD, a floppy disk or what."

"He had a set of really nice, leather-bound journals. I'm not positive, of course, but I think he might have written the list in one of those."

"That helps a little. Now, drink up." He waited until she'd taken a big gulp of her drink before continuing. "Now, is there anywhere in the hotel we haven't searched?"

Taking another sip, she considered. "There is one place," she said reluctantly. "I haven't been able to search there because Evan locked me out. I have a dance studio in the building out by the spa."

He raised his brows. "I don't know which is more surprising, that you have a dance studio or that Evan locked you out."

"He had his petty pleasures." Ignoring the heat coloring her face, she frowned at him. "Why would you be surprised I had a dance studio?"

"I didn't know you still danced."

"I do. Or did." She let out a big puff of air. "Even though I couldn't perform, I talked Evan into building me a dance studio here at the hotel. I told him I needed it to keep in shape."

Dom nodded. "If he locked you out, I can only assume the police haven't searched there?"

"No. No one's been in there for months. Not even Evan. After he locked it up, he made me watch him flush the key down the toilet."

"Rachel, why didn't you tell me?"

She shrugged. "I didn't think they could be in there. We can't get in without calling a locksmith. And I didn't want you to know how truly bad things were." Her excuses sounded lame even to her, now that she'd voiced them aloud.

"Hell of a life we've both had," Dom spoke, his tone

oddly gentle. "Show me the studio, Rach. There's not a lock invented that I can't pick. One of my special talents, just like Seb can break any code."

"What is it about your family?" she asked. "I know your father was in the Secret Service and your grandfather with the CIA. Seb's Special Forces. What about your sister?"

"Lea works for a large private firm. Currently, she's working in Europe, but Seb mentioned she was coming home to see Phillip."

"And you were FBI. That's amazing."

"Not so much." The bitter twist of his mouth shut her down. "I'm the black sheep of the family. My family has been in the spy business since the Civil War, and never has a Cordasic disgraced the family name. Until me."

Her heart ached, making her long to comfort him, though she knew she had no right to. "Phillip's words?"

He gave a brusque nod. "Now, about your dance studio. I'm willing to bet that's where Evan hid the list. His big production of flushing the key sounds designed to keep you out and he could have had a copy for himself. And it's the only place we haven't checked."

"This way." Accepting his change of subject, she started walking. When they reached the spa area, she led him around to the back. "The door is glass, but he had iron burglar bars installed on it. He also put on a heavy duty deadbolt, which can only be opened by a key."

"Or this." Grinning, he withdrew an odd-shaped tool from his pocket. "My plug." He inspected the lock briefly. "Now watch. If the bolt is protruding to the left, then I rotate the plug clockwise. If it's to the right, counter-clockwise. Simple as that."

The lock clicked. Dom stepped, back, gesturing at the door. "Go ahead. It's unlocked."

For the first time since she'd gotten the call about Jillie, she felt the cold knot in the pit of her stomach loosen. "Amazing," she murmured, stepping around him to open the door.

Once inside, she flicked on the light and felt a flash of comfort. She'd always loved the aesthetic lines of the space she'd created for herself. The mirrored wall reflected the mats and ballet barres.

Dom paused near the balance beams. "Gymnastics, too? Without waiting for an answer, he ran one large hand down the smooth wood. "Nice."

"Thanks." She gestured around the room. "But as you can see, there aren't many places here to hide anything."

"True, but I'm betting the list is here, somewhere."

"Right under my nose, all along. Evan really never came in here, you know. He didn't like to be reminded of what I was."

"Why else would he have such a lock installed on the door? He wasn't just locking you out, he was protecting his precious list." Dom raised his head, his dark brown eyes steady. "If I'm right, this will all be over. I'm sure whoever has been threatening you is on this list, too."

"That almost sounds too good to be true." She took a deep breath. "Well then, go ahead and search."

He began by inspecting the balance beams for hidden openings. He checked under the mats, and inspected the barres. Nothing.

Opening the cabinet under her little sink, he pushed aside her makeup and hairspray and deodorant. "Nothing," he announced, sounding disgusted. "But it's got to be here somewhere."

Watching while he perused the contents of her mini-fridge and wet bar, she managed to choke down her drink. Worrying about her son eclipsed her need to find the list, though the two were closely entwined.

Find the list and eliminate the threat to Cole.

Find the list and clear her name.

Find the list and send Dominic back out of her life.

Shaking her head, she tried to imagine never seeing him again. She'd forgotten—or forced herself to forget—his effect on her. He'd always seemed larger than life, more masculine than other men, dominating a room merely by walking into it.

Dominic. The man she should have married, would have married, had Evan Adair not walked into a show and decided Rachel should be his. She'd given up Dominic to save her sister and mother, but she'd never, ever forgotten him. She knew his body, every curve, every sinew and hollow. Everything about him turned her on. The masculine growl of his voice. The heat in his eyes every time he looked at her. The spread of his large, masculine hands. Even his feet. Watching him now, she found herself admiring the way he planted his large shoes when he stood.

They belonged together. How in the world was she going to have the strength to let him go?

Whistling under his breath, Dom continued searching.

Finally, when he came to the last thing in the room, the metal and plastic towel container and hamper, he felt along the edge and let out a low whistle. "I think I found it."

She moved closer, trying to see. "What did you find?"

"A false bottom. I'm working on figuring out how it opens."

Amazed, she crouched down beside him. "I've never noticed that, and I used that thing every time I came in here."

Something clicked. Dom slid the bottom sideways, flashing her a triumphant grin. "Jackpot." He held up three slim, leather-clad notebooks.

She smiled back, unable to resist. Reaching out her hand, she touched the embossed letters. *Evan Adair.*

"Open them up." Dom handed them to her. "Make sure they're what we're looking for."

Slowly, hesitantly, she opened the first notebook. The soft leather spoke of quality and care. Inside she saw Evan had, in his usual meticulous way, made an index, with headings and page numbers. When she flipped to the first section, she saw lists of transactions, items, cash that had traded hands. Names.

"There are lists of actual names." She could hardly believe it. "And each list is under a detailed description of illegal activity."

"I can't claim to know what Evan was thinking when he did that."

"He couldn't help himself." Continuing to page through the book, she shook her head. "I knew Evan had OCD. Everything is here."

"We did it, Rach!" Sweeping her up in his arms, Dom slanted his mouth over hers and stole a fierce, celebratory kiss. "With this list, the police will have no choice but to consider other suspects."

Immediately stiffening, she glanced at the camera. Following the direction of her gaze, Dom cursed under his breath.

She moved a safe distance away. "What about Nathan and the FBI? I don't want to turn the list over to them. I don't trust him."

"Neither do I. Nope." He touched his mouth, his gaze full of regret. "We go to the police with this."

Staring down at the notebooks, at first she couldn't move. Then she looked up and met his gaze, holding out the notebooks to him. "I want you to take them, keep them safe."

Though he raised a brow, he didn't question her decision. Instead, he slipped off his jacket and wrapped the notebooks inside.

"Ready?" His expression revealed no hint of his thoughts. She nodded, realized she was clutching her purse the way a drowning victim clutched a rescue line, and forced herself to relax.

He didn't slip his arm around her shoulders on the way to the elevator and she was oddly disappointed. Though she knew she couldn't, she wanted to lean into him, to let herself rely on his familiar strength.

The piped-in elevator music seemed too loud, the ornate mirrored sides reflecting her pale unease. Dom, she thought with a trace of resentment, looked tan, relaxed, at home with himself and the world. Inherently strong, vital and too damn beautiful.

He caught her studying him and smiled, making her catch her breath. "Are you okay?"

Lifting her chin to hide her confusion, she nodded. "I'm fine."

"That's odd. You look like the world just imploded." The teasing edge to his voice coaxed a reluctant smile from her.

"In a way, it has," she said softly. Once she'd turned in

the list, this would be over. Dom would go back to his life and she would go back to hers. She could see the future stretching out bleakly in front of her.

The elevator reached the lobby. With a discreet chime, the doors opened. Instant noise—the electronic slot machines, the chatter of thousands of people—assaulted them, along with the ever-present tang of cigarette smoke. No matter how many filters she installed, she could never vanquish the scent.

Side by side, they headed down the main concourse, past the quarter slot area, toward her favorite casino bar.

"Look." Touching Dom's arm, she pointed. Nathan Frederick had just strolled into the High Stakes Lounge.

After a quick look at each other, they headed toward him.

Dom didn't even try to be cordial. "What are you doing here?"

False smile fixed on his face, Nathan turned. "I like to play Texas hold 'em. Care to join me for a game?"

The table he stood near had a one hundred dollar minimum bet.

"Sure." Reaching into his pocket, Dom pulled out his money clip and peeled off a bill.

Nathan's grin widened. "Put mine on my house account," he told the dealer.

The young man looked at Rachel. "Ma'am?"

"Is there a problem?"

"Yes. Mr. Frederick's house account has been frozen." He tapped his computer. "Come see."

Nathan shrugged, appearing unfazed. "Must be some sort of mistake."

Behind the desk, Rachel took a look at the screen, disbelieving her eyes. According to the notes, Nathan owed the Lone Star over fifty thousand dollars! And the account was more than ninety days delinquent.

As she was about to speak, Dom's cell rang. He checked the caller ID. "Sebastian."

He moved away, probably to keep Nathan from over-hearing. Answering, he listened intently, his expression fierce as he relayed the info to Rachel. "He has Cole and Jillie. They're catching the next flight here."

"Here?" Rachel froze. "Why here? Tell him to take Cole somewhere safe."

Dom covered the phone. "Your son's hysterical. Seems he's convinced himself the bad man's trying to kill you. Cole's insisting Seb rescue you, too."

Unaccountably, Rachel's throat clogged. "I want to talk to my son."

Dom relayed her request to his brother, then handed her the phone.

"Cole?"

"Mommy!" Just the sound of her little boy's voice brought tears to her eyes. "Where are you, Mommy?"

"Here, at the Lone Star. Waiting for you."

"Oh. Me and Aunt Jillie had a 'venture, just like we did when Dom drove us up the mountain."

She wiped her eyes with the back of her hand, struggled to keep the emotion from her voice. "Were you scared, honey?"

"No." He sounded proud. "Aunt Jillie said I did real good. I helped her when the bad guy shot her."

Rachel could hear her sister in the background, talking excitedly. "Let me talk to her for a second, okay?"

"Okay, Mommy. I love you." He handed the phone over before Rachel could say she loved him back.

"Rach!" Jillie squealed into the phone. "Why didn't you tell me about Dom's brother?"

"You don't sound too bad for someone who's been shot." Rachel chuckled, her emotions swinging a wild pendulum. "I assume everyone is treating you okay?"

"More than okay. And tell Dom he should have told me his brother is freakin' hot!"

In the background, Rachel heard Sebastian snort. That reaction was more than she'd seen from him the entire time he'd been in Vegas. "At least he's not taking you seriously."

"Oh, he will," Jillie warned. "Before all this is over, I promise you, he will."

Rachel let that one go. Apart from her engagement to Alan, her twin had always fallen in and out of infatuation at the drop of a hat. If Sebastian could hold out against the roaring freight train that was her sister, more power to him.

"Jillie? Thank you for saving Cole."

"Saving Cole?" Jillie sounded incredulous. "Heck, girl. Cole's the one who saved me." She dropped her voice an octave. "And Sebastian, of course. He came to my rescue by offering to let me tag along to Vegas with Cole."

"Back to Vegas?"

"Yes."

"Ulterior motive?" Slipping back into the shorthand speech she and her twin had used when they were younger, Rachel didn't have to wait long for Jillie's answer.

"Of course." Barely pausing for breath, Jillie fired off her next question. "What about you and Dom? Don't stammer."

Rachel blushed, glad Jillie couldn't see her. "We found the list."

"Awesome."

Next, Sebastian wanted to have another word with Dom. Rachel handed the phone back, still smiling. Dom gestured her to stand closer, placing the phone in between them so they both could hear.

Dom told Sebastian about their find. "Now Rachel doesn't have to worry about being the only suspect."

Seb snorted. "That's why the Feds pulled Nathan, not just because I called Paul Kinney. They had no hard evidence, so they had to get out. Either that, or look like complete fools."

Watching Nathan intently, Dom didn't bother to hide his savage smile. "That's odd. Nathan said they had enough to go to the D.A. and ask for an indictment."

"He lied." Sebastian swore. "Paul knew you were involved. He'd have given me a courtesy call by now if that were true."

Seb's myriad connections never ceased to amaze Dom. "Well, Nathan's here. I think maybe it's time he and I had a discussion."

"Go get 'em, little bro. I'll check in with you later."

As Dom dropped the phone back in his pocket, Nathan cleared his throat. "Congratulations, Rachel. From what I hear, everything's going well for you now."

She jumped. "True." Unaccountably nervous, she peered up at Nathan. "Now, about the ante for the card game. I'm sorry," she said. "But we won't be able to extend any more credit to you. You'll need to pay cash or you can't play."

For the first time, Nathan's perpetual look of faint

amusement disappeared. With a defiant glare, he flashed them a twisted smile. "That's all right. I didn't want to play here anyway. I'll take my business somewhere it's valued."

With that, he stalked off.

Dom laughed. "How much does he owe?"

"Fifty thousand."

"Wow." Dom whistled. "That's a chunk of change." Steering her away from the table and her employee, he waited to say more until they'd exited the casino floor. "I want to take the lists and make copies and put them in the mail. I'll send them certified overnight. That way everyone gets them at once."

"Who are you sending them to?"

He began ticking them off on his fingers. "Las Vegas Metro Police, the Regional FBI office. The District Attorney's office, the United States Attorney General's Office—"

"What? Why?"

"For your protection." Dom spoke quietly. "There were a few senators and congressmen on those lists. I also want to send a copy to the CIA."

She liked the plan. "What about the media?"

"Oh, they'll have a field day. But I want to give the authorities a chance to investigate first."

"What about Nathan? He knows we have it."

"So will his office, once I mail all the copies out."

Rachel swallowed. "What about Nathan's gambling debt? Obviously he has a problem."

"I wouldn't be surprised if he doesn't owe a lot more. I'm sure other casinos have extended him credit as well. The Lone Star's attorneys can begin collection procedures."

Rachel nodded. "I'll look into it. Let me show you

where a copy machine is set up. I'll stand guard outside the door to make sure the other employees know the room is off-limits while you're in there."

While Dom made photocopies and she blocked the door, she wondered why she didn't feel more excited, more jubilant, more…something. Thanks to Dom's help finding the list, for the first time she believed she might have a fair shot of proving her innocence and making a decent, normal life for herself and her child.

If she didn't continue to screw up.

She glanced at the big man in the small room behind her, completely intent on the copy machine. His stance emphasized his narrow hips and broad shoulders and his strong hands were tan against the white paper. Even in the stark, utilitarian setting of the copy room, he exuded masculinity. She ached to touch him again, even knowing she couldn't.

Making love with Dom had been more than a huge mistake. Like some sort of addict, she couldn't stop thinking about him, wanting him, craving more. She didn't know how she was going to manage saying goodbye.

Chapter 10

Sebastian, Jillie and Cole pulled into the Lone Star entrance shortly after dusk, looking to Rachel like a television commercial of the perfect family. Tall, dark, handsome father; beautiful, blond mother; adorable young child sleeping in the back seat. Rachel knew an instant of wishful envy, knowing she'd never have that now.

"Hey, bro." Sebastian hugged Dom, then included Rachel, too. "Cole's asleep. I'm not sure if you want to wake him or not."

As Rachel started forward, Sebastian nodded. "Let me get your sister and you and Dom get him."

While Sebastian helped Jillie out, supporting her while she adjusted her crutches, Dom went to the back door and lifted Cole out of the car. Rachel gave Jillie a quick, breathless hug before hurrying over to see her little boy. Lightly kissing his forehead, she blinked back tears.

"Let him sleep," she told Dom softly. "Do you mind carrying him upstairs so I can put him to bed?"

"Not at all," he whispered back.

One of the valets brought a wheelchair for Jillie and, once they got her settled, they turned to go in.

Unfortunately, people recognized Jillie before Rachel could sprint her inside. Flashbulbs popped and, despite the chair, a small contingent of brave and determined souls bore down on her asking for her autograph.

Sebastian moved to head them off. "She's just spent hours traveling, people. Give her a little space."

"It's all right." Smiling broadly, Jillie waved to her fans. "It'll just take a minute to sign a few pieces of paper."

Rachel's heart sank as she noticed a national network news reporter bearing down on them, a cameraman by her side. So far Rachel had managed to keep the media away through casino security, but out here they were fair game.

Quietly she signaled to a security guard, who stepped between the camera and their growing group. Rachel hoped they hadn't gotten enough footage for a story.

For the next several minutes Jillie signed and posed for photos, looking glowingly beautiful, even in her wheelchair. She laughed off questions about her injury, saying she cut herself on a nail and needed stitches rather than revealing it was a gunshot wound. Rachel noticed Sebastian couldn't take his eyes off her.

And judging from Jillie's heightened color, her sister was well aware of his intense regard.

Cole managed to sleep through it all.

Finally, they reached the private elevator and headed up to the thirteenth floor. After getting Cole tucked into bed, Rachel rejoined the others in her sitting area.

Dominic patted the couch beside him. Frowning, Rachel shook her head and took the remaining chair.

"What's up between you two?" Jillie asked frankly. "I can practically feel the heat sizzling between you, but you act like you're afraid to touch."

"Jillie!" Rachel felt her face flare red. "Quit."

"No, I'd like to hear it, too." Sebastian rested his elbows on his knees, chin in his hands. "Being around the two of you for five minutes is making *me* jumpy, and I'm never jumpy."

"We can't all be as emotionally contained as you are," Rachel snapped.

Sebastian looked at Dom. "Does she know?"

"No." Dom laid his hand on his brother's arm. "Let's get off the personal stuff." The thread of warning in Dominic's deep voice ended that topic. "Let me fill you in on what's going to be happening around here soon." He outlined how he'd copied and overnighted the lists. "We kept the originals here."

Jillie continued to shoot Rachel worried glances. "Then what?"

"I've sent out a press release, announcing a news conference Friday at two. After that—" Dom leaned back against the couch "—all bets are off."

Sebastian's phone rang. He glanced at it and excused himself to take the call.

Rachel watched him leave the suite and yawned, though she was far too jumpy to be tired. "I'm thinking we ought to make it an early night."

Instantly, Dom stood, agreeing. Though his smoldering gaze felt like a touch, he made no move to come near her. "I'll go with Seb. We'll see you two ladies tomorrow."

The instant the door closed, Jillie rounded on her sister. "What is going on? You've slept with him, haven't you?"

Instead of trying to deny anything, Rachel gave a tired nod of her head and dropped onto her couch. "How could you tell?"

"Girl, you're glowing. So spill. If you and he have had sex, why are you acting like he has the plague?"

"It was only once. And won't happen again."

"Rachel, I've never seen you as happy as you were with him. You never told me why you left him for Evan to begin with."

"Threats. The same sort of thing when Evan wanted me to break off all contact with you and Mom. He kept showing up at my performances when I was dancing at Caesars Palace. I kept telling him I was engaged. One day he was waiting in my dressing room. He showed me a video of you, walking to class at the University of Texas. Then he described in vivid detail what would happen to you if I didn't break off my engagement and marry him. I didn't believe him at first."

Jillie touched her arm, letting her gather her composure. "But eventually, he did something to make you believe?"

"Yes. Remember when you were mugged that time on Sixth Street in Austin? Evan called it a prequel. The next time, he promised you'd be raped and severely beaten."

"That wasn't him." Jillie crossed her arms. "That was a random mugging."

"No, it wasn't. Evan arranged it. He promised to target Mom next."

"Oh, my God." Hand to her mouth, Jillie's eyes filled with tears. "Have you told Mom?"

"Not yet, but I will when this is all over. I haven't gotten ahold of her yet and now I'm glad. She'll want to come here, and I don't want her becoming a target."

"What about Dom? Does he know?"

"No. I don't want to give him a reason to hope for a reconciliation. He's the past. I've got to look toward the future."

"I'm guessing it's never occurred to you that your past might be your future?"

Rachel eyed her sister and sighed. "Let me tell you about Evan's will," she began. "Evan's will dictates that I can't have any relationship until Cole turns eighteen or Cole will lose all rights to his inheritance."

"What?" Jillie reared back. "You can fight this, I swear. I know a good lawyer—"

"No. I can't talk about it anymore." Rachel swallowed, pushing away the irrational terror that came at the thought of fighting any of Evan's decrees, even after his death. "Please. I've got enough on my plate right now." She looked at her sister, knowing she had to change the subject. "Now, Jillie, what's going on with you and Sebastian? I saw the way you looked at him. Are you and he...?"

"No." Jillie's expressive face lit up. "Not yet. But we will be, I can promise you that. He may not know it yet, but Sebastian Cordasic is mine."

Stunned, Rachel could only shake her head. "Good luck to you. He's a stand-up guy, so promise me you won't hurt him."

"I never hurt them." Jillie's blue eyes reflected puzzlement. "They're always the ones who want out. None of them have been able to handle my lifestyle."

Living in the shadow of one of America's favorite country music superstars couldn't be easy. Leaning over, Rachel hugged her twin. "I'm sorry. Do you want anything before we go to sleep?"

"No. Just show me my bed and I'll crash. Am I next door again?"

"I had a rollaway bed brought to my suite, so if you don't mind, you can stay here. After all that's happened, I think it'd be safer. Plus you'll need some help with clothes and stuff."

"Whatever." Jillie yawned. "About that bed…?"

"This way." Tired, Rachel yawned back.

Steering Sebastian down the hall toward his room, Dom glanced at his brother. "Did Rachel's comment bother you?"

"No. How could it? Nothing bothers me," Sebastian shot back, his even tone laced with a bitterness he claimed not to feel. "But when you get a chance, will you please let Rachel and her sister know about me? Not the details, just the outcome. I don't want to deal with more comments like that."

"Of course." Dom slugged Sebastian's arm. "Especially from Jillian, right? I've noticed how she looks at you."

"She's far too innocent for a man like me," Seb shook his head. "Don't even think it."

"Not to mention famous," Dom pointed out. "And completely out of your league."

"Yeah. Like Rachel is out of yours. Best remember that, little brother."

At the door to his suite, Dom stopped. "Are you ready to turn in?"

"Actually…" Sebastian hesitated, his expression once again his usual cold mask. "That was Phillip on the phone."

"Oh?" Using his card to unlock his door, Dom led the way inside. "How is he?"

"Still hanging in there." Sebastian headed straight for the in-suite bar and made himself a drink. He also got Dom a diet soda, splashing it over ice. "He called because he saw you on the news."

"When?"

"Just now. Must have been that whole mess when they spotted Jillie."

"So he saw me on TV. What'd he say?" Holding his breath, Dom waited.

"Remember what he said, how he might want you to come see him before the end, provided you weren't involved with Rachel?"

Dom knew what was coming. "Yes. And now you're about to tell me that, because he saw me with her on the news, I can forget about that."

"Not exactly. He said he wants to see you now."

"Really?" This was what he'd been working toward. Reconciliation, one last visit before his grandfather died. He should be ebullient, joyful. Instead, he felt like Sebastian. Dom felt…nothing. Not relief, not happiness, certainly not shock. He felt like his brother must feel every second of every day.

"That's promising," he said, cautiously.

"Wait, there's more." Sebastian's grim words confirmed Dom's suspicion. With Phillip, there was always a catch.

"He gave me a message to pass along to you. I don't agree with it, but then, I'm only the messenger."

Ah, here it came. Phillip fancied himself a bit of a puppeteer, always working the strings in his misguided attempts to manage his family.

"He's willing to write you back into his will—and he asked me to point out that each of us will receive fifty million dollars." Sebastian's voice reflected his distaste. Though the amount never changed, the dangling of the bequest was a regular tool Phillip utilized to keep the family in line.

"That's a chunk of change," Dom mused, as if on cue. All their lives, the entire family had talked about "the inheritance." Phillip himself had made certain no one forgot it, waving his wealth over them all like some kind of royal scepter he used to get them to do his bidding. Despite all that, Dom still loved the old man. Phillip honestly believed he was looking out for the good of the Cordasic family with his machinations.

Ironically, Dom hadn't talked about his potential inheritance with Rachel back when they'd been engaged. He wondered if it would have made a difference.

"And the catch? What does he want?"

"For once, I'm glad I can't feel anything." Mouth in a straight line, a muscle worked in Phillip's cheek. "When he says now, he means *now*. If you want back in his good graces, he wants you to pack and leave Vegas immediately."

"What? Rachel's case is nearly over. I can't leave *now*."

Sebastian gave a grim nod. "If you want to see Phillip, you have to quit."

"You know what? Retreat was the one thing I became good at after Rachel left me and then Raymond died. After that, I pretty much ran from everything." He took a deep breath. "One of the resolutions I made when I got sober was to stop running. I can't do this."

"It's your choice."

Not really, not his. Phillip's. His grandfather was demanding he run away from Rachel. Yet even though she'd told him in no uncertain terms it couldn't be, *they* couldn't be, he refused to give up. Not on her. Not on them. Even if doing so cost him his much-desired reconciliation.

Glancing up, he found Sebastian scrutinizing him.

"I think you know my answer," Dom said softly. "More than anything else in the world, I would have loved to see Grandpa Phillip before he died, but I can't do what he wants."

"Not more than anything else in the world." Sebastian's gravelly voice recited the facts, only the facts. "You want Rachel more."

"Yes." He acknowledged the truth of his brother's words with a wry smile. The one sentence summed up his life in a nutshell. *He wanted Rachel more.* She'd been the one good thing to ever grace his life and he refused to let her get away again.

"What about the inheritance?"

Dom shrugged. "Money isn't everything. Sometimes there are more important things in life." A point he had to prove to Rachel. He honestly believed Cole would be better off with Dom in his life than without him, inheritance or no inheritance.

"Do you think you have a chance with her?"

"I hope so." Dom smiled. "She still loves me. Maybe this time, love will win out over money."

"What do you want me to tell the old man?"

"Tell him this," Dom paused to take a deep breath. "No way in hell. Oh, and tell him I'll see him there." He wondered at his composure. "I'm going to bed. Since you always get up so early, I'll see you at six."

The next morning, Dom went looking for Jillie. He'd had enough of people getting hurt because of misconceptions.

He found her in the casino, long blond hair in a ponytail, wearing a Colorado Rockies cap and feeding quarters into a slot machine. Since few people stirred this early, the casino was fairly empty and no one had recognized her.

"Jillie." Coming up behind her, Dom laid his hand on Rachel's twin's shoulder. She swiveled around on her crutches. "I went to talk to you about Sebastian."

At the mention of his brother's name, her entire heart-shaped face lit up. "What about him?" she purred.

"You seem to like him."

She colored prettily. "Well, yeah. I can't believe I never met him when you and Rachel were together. I remember hearing about him, but I think he was in the military."

"He is. That's what made him the way he is now. He's seen things most of us never will, things we'd never want to see." He took a deep breath. "For the past year, he was a prisoner of war in the Middle East. He was rescued and sent home to recuperate. Offered an honorable discharge."

"You must be very proud of him."

"I am. The whole family is. But while he was held captive, things were done to him…"

Jillie's eyes went wide. "What kind of things? So help me, if you tell me they made him a eunuch…"

Now it was Dom's turn to stare. "A what? You mean, cut off his…? Hell, no."

Visibly relieved, she smiled. "Thank goodness. That would have been such a waste."

"True." He smiled back, then let his smile fade. "While Seb was a prisoner, they performed experiments on him. What they were, he says he doesn't remember. But they changed him. Sebastian cannot feel."

Her blank expression told him she didn't understand.

"When you say he can't feel…"

"Emotions. He can't feel anger. Regret. Sorrow. Happiness. Joy. Or…love."

She frowned. "How is that possible?"

"No one knows. The military doctors wanted to do tests on him. Seb refused. Then they decided his problem must be psychological. He refused to go to counseling. Lately, they've left him alone."

"Does Rachel know?"

"No. No one outside the family and the military know. You're the first person I've told."

Her thoughtful expression told him his words were beginning to sink in. "You keep talking about his job, about the military. What does he do in the military?"

"He was Special Forces." He scratched the back of his neck. "Our family's always been in intelligence, you know that. Whatever Sebastian did for the government is classified. Even now, he won't talk about it."

"I can understand that."

"You're a very public figure," he reminded her as gently as he could.

"You're warning me off." She glared at him, her blue eyes glacial. "You, of all people. I can't believe this."

"I don't want you to get hurt. You deserve to be loved. Sebastian can't give that to you."

She shook her head. "You're wrong, you know. Your brother *can* feel. Look how he helped Rachel out. And you— he's here for you. That means he must feel something."

"He says he knows what he's *supposed* to feel," Dom answered quietly, hating that he felt like he was breaking her heart. "He can fake the appropriate emotions when he needs to. But he no longer experiences them."

"For how long?" Now her blue eyes blazed. "Has he been given any sort of timeframe for when he can expect to return to normal?"

"No."

"It could happen tomorrow."

"Or never."

Jillie lifted her chin. "My glass is half-full. Yours appears to be half-empty."

Raising his hands, Dom gave up. "You win." He smiled. "If anyone can help Sebastian, I'm thinking you can."

"Thanks for the vote of confidence." She grinned back. "But you should know, I'm in it to win."

"For the long haul?"

She nodded. "Of course."

"Then take this into account, too. Sebastian makes his living by keeping to the shadows, while yours is all bright lights and public appearances. That could be more of a hurdle than the emotion problem."

"You know what they say." Jillie's grin widened. "Opposites attract." Blinking, she peered up at him. "Kind of like you and Rachel."

"She doesn't think so." He couldn't keep the glumness from his tone. "Once again, she thinks money is more important than me."

"She told me about Evan's will." Jillie cashed out her machine and took his arm. "It's completely natural for a mother to fight for her child's inheritance."

"But she isn't fighting." He couldn't contain his frustration. "She hasn't even attempted to contact a lawyer. No, this is a reenactment of before, when she left me for Evan. Money is more important to her than anything else."

She stared. "Is that what you really believe? That Rachel left you for Evan because he was rich?"

His eyes narrowed. "What do you know?"

Jillie began to pace. "My sister doesn't want you to know—she just told me all about it last night—but you were kind enough to tell me about Sebastian, so I might as well return the favor." Stopping, she studied him, her blue eyes glowing. "Plus, I truly believe you and Rachel belong together."

Suddenly dreading what he'd hear, he crossed his arms and he waited.

"Remember when I asked her what Evan did to make her cut off her family? How he threatened to hurt me and Mom?"

Dom nodded. And then his breath caught. "Are you saying Evan did the same thing to get her to break it off with me and marry him?"

"Exactly."

The crushing band he'd felt encircling his heart loosened. "Good thing Evan Adair is already dead."

Watching him, Jillie smiled. "Don't give up, Dom. I really believe you're the love of my sister's life and her one chance for happiness."

He grinned back. "I have no intention of giving up, Jillie. You can rest assured on that."

"Same here." She touched her mouth. "I'm not giving up on your brother, either. At least, not without a fight."

And she gracefully swung off on her crutches, leaving Dom thinking Seb wouldn't even know what hit him.

The calls started coming in at ten. The local markets first—television, radio and print. Rachel had her secretary relay the information about the press conference the next day, promising all questions would be answered then, at least to the best of her knowledge.

And now that the police and the Feds had their own copies, they probably knew more than she did.

The major media outlets, *Newsweek, People,* all the national network news stations, began phoning at eleven. They were given the same information as before—press conference tomorrow at two p.m. sharp.

But the one call Rachel worried about the most—the man who kept threatening Cole—didn't come. It was far past the deadline now, and she couldn't help feeling that not hearing from him was a bad sign.

At twelve-thirty, she and Cole met Jillie, Dom, and Sebastian for lunch at the Ranger Café by the pool. The instant he saw the others, Cole jumped up and down with excitement.

"Dom!" Pulling his hand free from Rachel's, Cole flung himself at Dominic. "Where've you been?"

Dom bent down to hug him back. "I've been right here, little guy. You were asleep when you got home last night. Are you going to do some cannonballs into the pool for me?"

Cole's bright blue eyes sparkled as he grinned, revealing one missing tooth. "Oh, yeah," he said fervently. "I'm really good at those."

"Don't I get a hug?" Jillie held out her arms. She wore a big floppy hat and huge sunglasses, an obvious attempt at disguise. Cole ran to her next, slowing to gently hug her without jostling her leg. Rachel's eyes teared up.

They sat at a round table, keeping the conversation light and inconsequential while they ate. Once they'd finished, Cole wanted to swim. Rachel compromised by letting him sit on the edge and splash until he'd had a chance to digest his food.

She waited until he was splashing happily before she brought up the caller. "Do you suppose he just went away now that we're making the list public?"

"Probably," Dom said. The smoldering flame she saw in his eyes made her heart skip, despite her determination not to let him affect her. He seemed larger than life, his vitality overflowing. He moved with restless energy, his masculine confidence making him even more attractive. Apparently, the upcoming events exhilarated him.

"Those kind of people don't usually just vanish," Sebastian warned, shooting his brother a hard look. "You should know that from your profiling classes at Quantico."

"Not usually." Dom lifted his chin, his expression confident. "But this guy wanted the list. Now he knows he can't have it. End of story. Besides, his name is most likely on it and, believe me, there are some prominent, well-known people's names. I doubt he'd want to draw attention to himself now."

For the rest of the day, it appeared Dom was right. Her cell didn't ring with threatening phone calls. Though she wanted the man caught, Rachel thought she'd settle for him going away. The list had been made public, after all, and whatever twisted game he'd planned to play had been thwarted.

Finally, the tension between her shoulders began to relax. That evening, as she walked Cole to her private elevator to get ready for bed, she thought she might have her first decent night's sleep in weeks. Sebastian and Dom were going over security for the press conference. Jillie had donned a new disguise and gone to play some slots, but she'd promised to meet Rachel in the suite shortly. Dom had wanted to walk Rachel to her suite but she had ignored the flash of hurt she saw in his eyes and waved him off, claiming exhaustion.

Cole couldn't stop yawning. When she mimicked him for a third time, he giggled. "Yawns are contagious," she told him. He nodded solemnly, blue eyes twinkling. They'd just turned the corner to her private elevator, when someone called her name. Turning, she saw Nathan Frederick hurrying toward her. From his bloodshot eyes to his rumpled suit, the FBI agent appeared disheveled, completely unlike himself.

"Thank goodness I found you," he said. "I need help."

Cole tightened his grip on her hand. The kid had good instincts, she thought.

"Is this about your account?" Pointedly, she glanced at her watch. "It's nine-thirty at night. Come talk to me in the morning, during normal business hours."

"No, no." He appeared frantic, gaze darting from her to the elevator to the deserted hallway. Rachel began to wish some guests would join them.

"I've had a car accident." Lifting his suit jacket, Nathan showed a crimson stain. "I think I really need your help."

"You need medical attention." Rachel flipped open her cell phone. "Let me call for an ambulance."

"I already did." Nathan grabbed her arm. "I think I might have killed someone. I panicked. I—I left their body under my car."

"You left the scene of an accident?" How could anyone, especially a by the book federal agent, be so stupid?

"I think I'm in shock." Nathan weaved. He stumbled, pulling on her and causing her to stagger.

Cole made a sound, his wide eyes and the tight grip on Rachel's hand telling her he felt the same unease.

Rachel kept her phone out. "Let me call someone from my staff to help you. I've got to get Cole to bed."

"Rachel, please. I'm a federal agent. I'm asking for your help. You're the casino owner. I'd hate to have to report to the news that I went to you for help and you declined. At least go with me to wait for the ambulance."

Already, she could picture the media frenzy and the lawsuit. She gestured toward the door leading outside.

"Where did this happen?"

"The south parking garage."

She nodded. Most of the locals used the south. It wouldn't be deserted and was well lit.

Outside, the heat hit her in a wave, as if she'd opened the door to a massive oven. Rachel stopped. Despite everything, her gut was telling her to turn around. From the way Cole was clutching her hand, he felt the same. She turned back toward the door.

"Where are you going?" Nathan sounded panicked.

"I'm going to take Cole back inside and leave him with my sister. He doesn't need to see this."

"No." Lunging, Nathan grabbed at her free arm. "We don't have time for that. What if this woman dies?"

"Let me go," Rachel ordered. "Right now."

Nathan dropped his hand.

Exhaling, Rachel turned again for the door, pushing Cole in front of her. Nathan moved, fast. She looked back just in time to see him coming at her with what looked like an old T-shirt. Then it was over her face. She smelled a sickly sweet odor and had just enough time to panic before everything went black.

Chapter 11

As they left the room where the press conference was to be held, Sebastian actually looked eager. "Let's go find Jillie."

Trying not to do a double-take, Dom looked again. It must have been a trick of the light, because his brother's normal, unruffled expression was back.

They found Jillie roaming the casino looking for them, wearing a brown wig and another hat. She looked up as they approached. While she gave Dom a wan smile, her pretty face briefly lit up at the sight of Sebastian. "Boy, am I glad to see you guys. I've been trying to find you for the last twenty minutes. I need your cell phone numbers so next time, I can call."

"What's wrong?" Dom asked.

"I went back to the suite to meet Rachel. She's not there. Neither is Cole." She took a deep breath, worry making frown lines in her forehead. "Nothing looks like it's been disturbed," she rushed on. "So I figured they must not have gotten there yet. But Rachel won't answer her phone."

"She seemed pretty tired." Sebastian crammed his hands in his pockets, glancing from Jillie to Dom. "Where would she have stopped?"

"That's the thing. I've searched the pool, her office, even the spa area. She's disappeared." Though her tone continued to be light, concern darkened her blue eyes.

Dom swore, earning a censoring look from two gray-haired ladies in matching polyester-slack sets. "Call the police. And let's check with security."

"But why?" Jillie grabbed his arm. "The crazy guy wouldn't have abducted Cole now. Everyone knows the list has gone out. They've got to be here somewhere."

"I don't know," Sebastian put in. "Like I tried to tell you earlier, this guy might be pissed because we didn't turn the list over to him. He might have decided to get revenge."

"If he's hurt Rachel or Cole..." Dom knew his furious expression finished his sentence for him.

Jillie punched 911 in her cell. As she spoke to the dispatcher, they saw flashing lights outside the south entrance.

"There." Dom took off, Sebastian close behind.

In the street in front of the Lone Star, three police cars, a fire truck, and an ambulance roared past.

Jillie caught up with them, clopping on her crutches, and waved her phone. "She said the police were already en-route."

"Where the hell are they going?"

"The parking garage." Again Dom took off at a run. Sebastian stayed behind, to help Jillie.

They caught up to Dom where a small circle of people

had clustered down near the end of row twelve. The convoy of emergency vehicles was there, too.

"Cole?" Jillie asked. When she tried to push forward, Seb grabbed her.

"Easy. Take it easy."

Dom moved ahead of them, pushing his way through the onlookers. It wasn't Cole on the pavement, blood pooling under his head. It was Rachel. Dom dropped to his knees beside her, feeling for a pulse. Cole was nowhere in sight.

On the way to the hospital, Rachel regained consciousness. She screamed for Cole as she remembered what had happened, and fought the ambulance attendants, furious when they restrained her. "Where's my son?" she asked, over and over. "Let me go. I've got to find my son."

As the only family member, Jillie had been the only one allowed to ride in the ambulance with her. "We'll find him, Rachel." She sounded soothing, though Rachel wasn't buying it. "Don't worry. Dom and Seb will find him."

"Call Dom," Rachel ordered. "Tell him it was Nathan all along. Nathan's the one who did this. He's the one who took Cole. If he finds Nathan, he'll find my son."

"We'll tell him when we see him at the hospital."

"What if Nathan hurts Cole?" Rachel wailed. "I don't understand why he did this. He knows we went public with the list."

"I'm sure Cole's all right," Jillie murmured, looking almost as close to losing it as Rachel. "He's only five. Surely this Nathan won't hurt such a small child."

But they both knew the world was full of people who would and could and did.

As they roared into the hospital's emergency entrance, Rachel's phone rang. Jumping, at first she stared at it. Caller ID showed an unfamiliar number.

"Hello?" She heard her own voice, high-pitched and anxious.

"Rachel?" It was Nathan. "I think I have something of yours." Even his laugh sounded different. More confident and full of power.

"Put Cole on," she ordered. "I want to talk to my son."

"Not until we discuss—"

"No." Interrupting him, she tried to sit up, nearly blacking out. "I'm not discussing anything until I hear his voice."

Then to her immense relief, she heard Cole's voice on the phone. "Mommy? Will you please tell Agent Frederick to bring me home?"

"Cole, you're all right." Sobbing, she gripped the phone, conscious of the ambulance attendant and Jillie staring at her.

"Not for long." Nathan again. In the background, she could hear her son calling for her, ripping out her heart.

"Nathan, why are you doing this?"

"Listen to me now. If you ever want to see your son alive again, you'd better take notes."

"I don't have paper. I'm in an ambulance."

The ambulance stopped in front of the emergency entrance. The attendants gestured to her phone. "You'll have to call him back."

"But—" Everything spun. Nathan continued talking, Jillie said something, and the attendant again cautioned her to turn off her phone.

Dominic and Sebastian rushed over.

"Nathan did this," Jillie said. "She's talking to him now."

Dominic snatched the phone from Rachel, talking low and furious. Though he followed close behind as the paramedics rushed Rachel inside, she couldn't hear what he said. She glanced back and saw that Jillie and Sebastian were right behind him.

The paramedics took her into the back, leaving the others in the waiting room and Jillie to fill out the necessary paperwork.

They took X-rays and determined Rachel had a concussion from her fall to the pavement. No surprise there. She also had some cuts and abrasions, all minor. The doctor, a nice man with a long gray ponytail, wanted to keep her overnight for observation.

Of course, she adamantly refused.

They worried over her rapid heart rate until she snarled at them to leave her alone. She couldn't tell them the reason any more than she could call the police or the FBI.

No matter what, she *had* to save her son.

They let Jillie back into her room while Rachel waited for the release paperwork.

"Where's Dom?" Rachel couldn't help looking for him. "I need to know what Nathan said."

"They're still in the waiting room." Jillie touched Rachel's bandaged head. "How badly do you hurt?"

"They gave me something for the pain. I'm okay as long as I don't touch the back of my head. Nathan used chloroform to knock me out, but I can't believe he just let me fall."

"I guess he was too busy kidnapping Cole." Jillie took a deep breath. "Listen, I called Mom. She wanted to catch a flight here immediately, but I think I talked her out of it."

Rachel nodded, then winced as pain shot through her head. "Once I get Cole back, I definitely want her to come."

"You need to tell her that yourself. She's hurt that she hasn't connected with you."

"I know. And I tried to call her once. But I haven't since then—I didn't want her coming out here and putting herself in danger. You know how absentminded she is." Glancing at her watch, Rachel sighed. "How long does preparing release papers take? We need to go."

"Here." Jillie handed over her cell phone. "Hit redial. Mom's waiting for your call."

Accepting the phone, Rachel hesitated. "Did you tell her what's going on?"

"Yes. She only wants to make sure you're okay."

Unaccountably nervous, Rachel punched the redial button and hit send. A second later her mother answered.

"Hi, Mom." Her throat tightened and her eyes filled with tears. "I'm all right. I'll be better once I get Cole back." She gave an abbreviated version of the last couple of weeks, reassuring her mother that she didn't need to buy a plane ticket yet. "I'll see you soon. I love you, too."

She handed the cell back to Jillie. "That felt good," she said. "I've really missed her."

From the glint in Jillie's eyes, Rachel could tell she was about to deliver a lecture, but a nurse arriving with paperwork spared Rachel from that.

Once everything had been signed, the nurse departed. Jillie helped Rachel dress.

"Do you need me to help you walk?"

Rachel shot her sister a warning look. "I hurt my head, not my legs. Plus, you're the one on crutches."

Jillie lifted her hands in mock surrender. "Sorry. I thought you might be dizzy from whatever pain meds they gave you."

Instantly abashed, Rachel gave her a hug. "Don't pay any attention to me. I'm worried sick about Cole."

The instant they rounded the corner into the waiting room and she spotted Dom heading toward her, she nearly tripped in her impatience to get to him.

"Easy." He steadied her. "You don't want to fall again."

She waved away his concern. "I won't. Dom, what did Nathan say to you? What does he want? Why'd he kidnap Cole?"

"Shhh." Handing her back her cell, he glanced around the waiting room.

"But—"

He brushed a kiss on her forehead as he took her arm. "We'll talk about this once we get out of here. I don't want random people to overhear. Are you ready?"

"Definitely." It took all the self-control she had not to lean into him. Even standing close, the strength and warmth of his large body comforted her. To distract herself, she looked for Jillie. Her sister and Sebastian stood close together near the doorway, heads bent together while they talked.

With Dom at her side, Rachel left the hospital. Jillie and Seb followed.

Once they were in Dom's pickup, she asked again. "Well? Tell me. What do I have to give Nathan to get Cole back?"

He started the truck, backing from the spot before answering.

"Nathan wants two million dollars." Dom's voice was completely without inflection. "Since the list is now public, he no longer cares about it. Evidently the reason he wanted it before was to blackmail people for money. Since that's no longer possible, he wants the money from you."

"Why?" Jillie sounded bewildered. "I thought this Nathan guy was FBI. He's a federal agent, not a crook, right?"

Sebastian chuckled, surprising them all. "It's possible to be both, you know. Most criminals have their own justification for their actions. I'm sure Nathan has one, too."

"Gambling debts," Dom put in grimly. "He owes the Lone Star fifty grand. No doubt he owes every casino on the strip at least that amount."

"When?" Rachel asked. "When does he want this money?"

"Immediately. He said he'll check in with you every hour on the hour, but he's given you twelve hours to come up with two million dollars."

"Twelve hours? I can't get that kind of money in that length of time. I don't know that I could raise two million dollars in a month, never mind half a day. Nathan especially should know that." Rachel regarded him helplessly. "Everything's tied up in probate. Right now, the only money I can access is operating funds to keep the Lone Star running."

"What about the casino vault?" Jillie asked. "You have a key to that, don't you?"

Staring at her sister, Rachel slowly nodded. "How do you know about that?"

Jillie shrugged. "I watch TV."

"That would be illegal," Sebastian said.

"Who cares?" Jillie and Rachel replied in unison.

Sebastian's brows rose. "I didn't say I wouldn't do it, just pointed out the obvious. I should also tell you that kidnapping is a federal crime. We need to call the FBI."

"And of course you know Nathan said if we did, he'd kill Cole," Dom said. "Which is why I held Seb off until we spoke to you. I don't think Nathan will hurt Cole, because then he'd lose his bargaining chip, but you never know. He sounded desperate."

"We can't take the chance." Rachel looked Seb full in the face. "No police, no Feds. Agreed?"

Slowly, he nodded. "Back to the vault, then. How much money do you keep in there?"

"I don't know. The key was Evan's. I never had much to do with the casino until he died. I've been learning as I go."

"I'm sure there's at least a million." Jillie's smile was full of hope. "If we had more time, I could free up some of my assets and raise the cash for you, but that would take more than twelve hours. I'd be perfectly happy to do it, though. Maybe you should ask him for more time."

"He's unstable. The longer he has Cole, the more we risk Cole getting hurt."

Rachel set her jaw. Dom was right. "I'm not taking the chance. The only thing I'm going to ask Nathan for is to give me back my son."

"Maybe Dominic can help with that." This came from Seb. "He's a damn good hostage negotiator."

"Was," Dom pointed out sharply, gripping the steering wheel. "Not anymore."

"We won't need a negotiator." Now Rachel was the one touching his arm, offering comfort. "We'll do this as a team, and quickly. Find the money, get Nathan paid, get Cole back."

"I'll help you," Jillie vowed. "Let me make some phone calls and see how much I can raise."

"Rachel." Sebastian's deep voice made Rachel turn. "You shouldn't pay him anything."

"What?" Rachel couldn't believe he'd said that. "Are you crazy? Of course we're going to pay him. He's got Cole."

"No. Ask Dom. Standard procedure. You don't ever pay the kidnapper. Once you do, you lose your one piece of power over them and they kill the hostage."

She looked at Dom. He nodded. "Seb's right. I've seen it happen time and time again."

"I don't care about procedure," she snapped. "All I care about is Cole. And Nathan *is* FBI. He knows the deal just as well as the two of you do. He kidnapped Cole for money. He has no reason to hurt him once he's paid."

Sebastian dipped his big head. "If you do what he wants, he'll kill your son. Because of this, he's already lost his job. If he's caught, he'll go to prison. And putting a federal agent in prison with people he helped convict is worse than a death sentence. Nathan has nothing to lose." He might have been discussing the weather, for all the emotion in his voice.

"What the hell is wrong with you?" Turning on him, Rachel realized her hands were balled up into fists. "How can you sound so uncaring? Don't you give a damn about anything?"

Jillie gasped. "Rachel!"

But Sebastian met her gaze, his own clear and unapologetic. "I am what I am. I was merely stating the facts."

Rachel wanted to bare her teeth, to hit something,

anything to make her feel less powerless. Instead, she stared straight ahead, her throat tight, eyes aching.

"Let it go, Rach," Dom said. "Sebastian has his own issues, and they have nothing to do with this. We'll come up with a plan to save Cole."

"No police. No FBI. I can't *not* pay him, not if there's a chance to save my son."

"Let's get back to the Lone Star. The clock's ticking. We can't take a chance on missing the deadline."

Once back at the hotel, Rachel immediately wanted to check the vault. "There are security cameras, but I need to see how much is in there."

"Bad idea." Dom touched her shoulder. "With the list out and the press conference scheduled tomorrow morning, you know they'll be watching you like a hawk."

"I don't care."

"Do you want the police to show up and take you in for questioning?"

"What do you mean? Those are my employees monitoring the cameras."

"I'm sure the police have someone on the inside, just in case. Feds, too. They usually do."

Rachel crossed her arms. "Then what do we do? I've got to get the money somehow."

Dom pulled her close. For once, she didn't care who saw. "Sebastian is right, you know. Once you turn over the money, there's nothing to stop Nathan from killing Cole."

"Oh, God. Do you really think he'll do that?"

He kissed the top of her head. "We won't let him."

Rachel breathed in his scent, drawing from his strength.

Across the room, Jillie met her gaze. In the way of twins, she knew her sister was thinking the same thing as she. What would Rachel do without Dom? How could she bear to tell him goodbye?

Seb cleared his throat. "Now all we need is Nathan to keep his word. He said he'd call back in an hour."

"I know." Rachel glanced at the clock. "It's past time. He should have called by now. It's twelve minutes past."

"He'll call."

"He'd better not have hurt Cole." Taking a deep breath, she willed herself calm. "Where do you think he's taken my son?"

"Someplace close," Dom said. "Sebastian's working on finding out."

"I've made contact with the cell phone provider." Sebastian held up his own phone. "Since Nathan is calling Rachel on her cell, I'm trying to find out if we can track his location that way." He turned away, punching numbers into his phone. Back to them, he began speaking in a voice too low for them to hear.

"Rach?" Dom brushed her hair away from her face. "I've done some checking. Nathan owes the other casinos over half a million dollars."

As distractions went, that was a good one. "That's surprising. To think I was worried about the measly fifty thousand he owes the Lone Star."

"He actually owes much more than that. I checked Evan's list. Nathan's name was in there. He owes your casino well over a hundred grand."

Sebastian turned around and gave a thumbs up. "We're ready. Now all we need is him to call."

As if on cue, her cell phone rang.

"Keep him on the line as long as possible," Sebastian said. "They need time to track the call."

Heart pounding, she nodded and answered her phone. "Hello?"

"Have you got my money yet?" Nathan.

Glancing at Dom, she swallowed. "Let me talk to Cole."

"No. He's finally fallen asleep. I was about to gag him," Nathan mocked, wrenching her heart, "just to stop the incessant crying for Mommy. You know…" His voice turned confidential. "I've never liked kids, never wanted any. That's one of the reasons I never got married."

Rachel didn't pretend to care. "I'm working on getting the money."

"You don't have too much time."

She glanced at Sebastian, who gestured to her and mouthed, "Keep him on the line."

"What are you going to do with two million dollars anyway, Nathan? I know you owe a lot of casinos money, but even once you pay them—"

"To hell with paying them," Nathan interrupted. "Once I get my money, I'm going to disappear to a place where I can live a life of leisure."

"Changing your identity?"

He laughed. "Already taken care of. I'm going to build a fortress on some island and surround myself with beautiful women, premium liquor and luxurious toys. With that much money, I won't have to answer to anyone."

"Two million won't last long." Rachel saw Dom frown. "Sorry." She shrugged, mouthing, "I don't know what else to say."

"Careful or I'll up the amount," Nathan said. "Time's a-wastin', Rachel. You'd better get busy." He disconnected the call.

"I think we got it." Seb talked into his own phone. "We'll know in a few minutes."

"I can't believe you said that, Rachel." Jillie chewed her bottom lip nervously. "Even though two million isn't a fortune, Nathan will still have enough to run far and fast."

"And with his government resources, he can disappear before anyone even realizes he's missing," Dom added. "Knowing him, I'll bet he's planning to screw the casinos, and forget about his debt. He'll have a new name, a new location and money. A new life."

"You're exactly right." Rachel began to pace, needing to expend her nervous energy. "He was calling to check on my progress. He wouldn't let me talk to Cole—he said he was asleep."

Dom and Sebastian exchanged a glance. "That's not good. Next time, tell him either you talk to your son or he doesn't get the money."

"But—"

"Rach, you've got to give him a reason to keep Cole alive." Dom hated to speak so bluntly, but she needed to understand.

Her eyes widened. "Oh, God. You don't think he's hurt him, do you?"

"Of course not." Jillie glared at Dom. "Don't get her even more upset and worried."

Grim-faced, Rachel nodded. "I think it's time we go to the vault. I need to see how much money is in there."

"Not yet." Sebastian held up his hand, speaking again

into his phone. "Jackpot. We've found him. Nathan's holed up at the Silver Star downtown."

"So close." Rachel looked up at Dom. "Now what?"

Dom released her. "Now we're going to rescue Cole."

"How? I don't have the money yet."

The two men exchanged a long glance, making her nervous.

"Forget about the money," Seb told her. "Dom and I are going in."

"Going in?" Rachel echoed, looking from Dom to Seb. "What do you mean, going in?"

"We're going to take him by surprise," Seb answered. "Overwhelm him commando style and snatch your son."

"What?"

"Don't worry. Hostage rescue is what I do—did—in the military. My successful missions number in the double digits, under much more dangerous conditions. This will be a snap."

Chapter 12

"That's your plan? To storm in and take him?" Rachel said. "Absolutely not."

She stepped forward, placing herself squarely in Sebastian's path. "No way in hell am I letting you do this. If you force your way into Nathan's room, he'll shoot my son."

Dom tended to agree with her. He'd seen too many rescue attempts go bad. But Seb was good and if anyone could rescue Cole this way, he'd bet on his brother.

"I have the element of surprise on my side," Sebastian argued. "He won't be expecting this."

But when Jillie moved to close ranks with her sister, Seb shook his head and raised his hands. "Fine. You win. Let's at least go over to the Silver Star and see what we can find out."

Dom touched Rachel's arm. "It couldn't hurt."

When she looked at him, the raw agony in her eyes tore at his heart. "All right," she whispered hoarsely. "Let's go."

When they arrived at the Silver Star they stared in shock. The Metro Police SWAT unit had preceded them. Black-suited SWAT members were involved in a furious debate with the Feds. Dom counted seven LVMPD police cars, two ambulances and a fire truck.

All the major networks were there as well with their news vans, live satellite feeds, and continuous coverage. The news anchors, perfect hair in place, were grabbing anybody and everybody for on-the-scene interviews, their cameramen trailing behind.

The Silver Star resembled a chaotic circus.

"Great," Dom groaned, shooting a censuring glance at his brother. "Look what you've done."

"I didn't call them," Sebastian said grimly. "Maybe Nathan called the media and they called the police."

"But Nathan's the one who said no police." Rachel clutched Jillie's arm. "And I really don't think he'd want the police or the Feds here."

Jillie frowned. "If Nathan didn't, and we didn't who did? How'd they find out?"

Dom looked at Sebastian. "The cell phone company. There must be a leak there."

"Great." Rachel sounded on the verge of hysteria. "What if Nathan sees? He'll think we did this."

"There's nothing we can do to change things." Dom tried to sound soothing. "Nathan will realize that, too. He won't hurt Cole. He needs him to get what he wants."

"He's holding all the cards right now," Sebastian added,

his unemotional voice strangely soothing. "But only as long as his hostage is alive."

Visibly shaken, Rachel finally nodded.

"When is Nathan supposed to call you?" Dom asked.

She glanced at her watch. "We've got fifteen minutes."

One of the news crews spotted them and pointed. Waving a microphone, the reporter ran toward them, suit coat flapping, camera crew right behind.

"Come on." Sebastian took off, Jillie limping close on his heels. She'd ditched the crutches. Holding Rachel's arm, Dom pulled her after them.

Sebastian flashed an ID and one of the Feds standing guard let them through a roped off area. He squinted at Dom as they passed, no doubt trying to remember where he'd seen him. Since the lanky man looked familiar, Dom wouldn't have been surprised to learn they'd worked together in the past.

"Hurry," Seb urged.

Passing through a set of doors that led to the kitchen, they crossed that room and exited on the other side, ending up in a hallway with elevators marked Employees Only.

"How'd you engineer that?" Jillie quirked one perfectly shaped eyebrow in question.

"It's all about connections." Sebastian wasn't bragging; he simply stated the truth. "They think I've been sent here."

Dom stared at his brother. "Sent here how?"

"They think this is my mission." Without waiting for their reaction, Seb turned away. He rummaged in his backpack before straightening. "And it was, though unofficially. At least until you guys axed the plan."

"We've got to come up with another strategy," Rachel said, sounding more composed and determined. Jillie seconded her.

Seb looked at Dom and said nothing. Dom knew what Seb thought he should do. But he couldn't. What if he screwed up again?

"It's your call," Dom told Rachel, crossing his arms. "If you have a better idea than Seb's, let's hear it. We came here to get Cole. With the media circus outside, you know Nathan is aware he's surrounded. Whatever we do, we've got to come up with something fast."

In the brief silence while she pondered, Dom could hear the slow, steady beat of his heart.

When Rachel's gaze came up to study his face, his heart skipped a beat.

"You're a hostage negotiator," she said. "A damn good one, too. Dom, talk to him. Talk Nathan into releasing my son."

He felt the blood drain from his face. This was what he'd feared. "I'm not—"

"You are." Her voice was firm. "Dom, you can talk to him. Make him give up."

Apprehension knotted inside him. He wished he could believe it would be that easy. Rachel had no idea what she asked of him, no idea that by trusting him, she might be endangering her beloved son.

"I don't—" Dom swallowed, inhaled, tried again. "I'm no longer a negotiator."

The obstinate set of her chin told him she wasn't listening.

"Honestly, Rachel. I haven't done that kind of work

in years, not since Raymond died." Maybe if he reminded her of what had happened, she'd realize he spoke the truth.

"Please." Rachel begged. "For Cole. For me."

Dom turned to his brother, looking for help.

But Sebastian just nodded. "I think it's a good idea."

Jillie watched silently, her expression encouraging. Dom knew she remembered how his partner had died.

"I don't think I can," he finally admitted, hoping Rachel would understand.

"Not even for Cole?" Rachel still eyed him expectantly.

"Especially for Cole." Saying the words felt like they'd been ripped from him. Dom couldn't take the chance of failing again, of being responsible for the actions of another madman. Especially when Cole's life hung in the balance.

"Talk him down." Sebastian's order penetrated Dom's frozen horror. "Do what you're trained to do, little brother. Negotiate. Do your thing."

Crisis. He felt himself go into lockdown. How could he gamble on something so precious, both to him and the woman he loved? Two innocent children, a woman and his partner had died because he'd failed. If he were to fail now…the consequences would be unspeakable. "No. I can't."

Fist to her mouth, Rachel turned her terrified gaze his way. The pain and accusation in her eyes skewered him. "Can't?" she rasped. "Or won't?"

He spoke the words no good hostage negotiator even thinks. "What if I fail?"

"You've got to try." Rachel touched his arm. "No matter what happened to you in the past, try now. For me. For Cole."

For Cole. But in his mind's eye he kept seeing that other

little boy and his sister, that terrified woman with a drunk madman holding a gun to her head. Ray, Dom's partner, cursing under his breath while Dom tried to do as he'd been trained: talk slow and steady.

The gunman blew the woman's brains out first. The kids started screaming. Raymond had run in first, and following behind him—too slowly—Dom had seen in the gunman's flat, dead eyes what he meant to do. As Ray leapt forward in a futile attempt to save the boy, the gunman killed them both— Ray and his son, two fast shots—then turned the gun on his little girl, killing her before the snipers took him down.

The blood had been awful. The pain, even worse. So much carnage. So much death. All his fault.

Knowing this, knowing he'd been responsible, how could Rachel want him to try and save her son?

Sebastian, understanding Dom's inner turmoil, put his arm around him. "Dom, you know this is not the same, not even close. You know this man. Nathan is—*was*—FBI. He trained at Quantico, like you. You know how he thinks. You can do this."

Stomach knotted, Dom looked at them all. Finally, he gave them a bleak, tight-lipped smile. "Rachel, are you sure you want to put your son's life in my hands?"

Without hesitation, she nodded. "Yes. There's no one I trust more." Standing up on tiptoe, she kissed him full on the mouth. Her extraordinary eyes glowed with confidence.

His breath caught in his throat. Finally, slowly, he nodded. "Let's go."

Sebastian led the way. The Feds had set up a miniature command center in one of the suites. He took them there, gesturing for them to set Dom up with a phone. But before they could, Rachel's cell phone rang.

Dom froze, then took her phone. "Hello, Nathan," he said.

"Evidently Rachel isn't good at following directions," Nathan snarled. "This place is surrounded. Tell her she's made a foolish mistake. She's going to pay for this."

Before Dom could speak, Nathan disconnected the call.

"He hung up," Dom said. "I'm going to call him back." Hesitating only for a moment, he pulled out a chair. Then, palms sweaty, he punched the button for incoming calls and hit dial. Blood roaring in his ears, he glanced once more at Rachel, waiting for Nathan to pick up his cell.

"What do you want, Rachel?" Nathan snarled when he finally answered. "Your kid is tied up and gagged and, from the look of him, has gone into shock. Do you want me to make it worse?"

"It's not Rachel," Dom said, glad she hadn't had to hear. "Just me, Dominic Cordasic."

Nathan laughed. "They're using you as a negotiator? The most highly touted failure in all of the Bureau, and they picked you to try and talk me into giving up? They must really want to fail."

"I don't work for the FBI anymore, remember? They don't know I'm calling," Dominic said. "I called to warn you. My brother is trying to talk the LVMPD out of sending a SWAT team to storm your room."

"That would be stupid." Nathan's tone became somber. "You forget, I know all the tricks. They won't use brute force, not yet. Doing so would be against every rule we were taught at Quantico. You always give the perp a chance to give up on his own, remember?"

Dom sighed, as though exasperated. Though he could hear his blood roaring in his ears, his voice sounded steady. "Oh, I know. They do, too, but they don't care. They've got the list, Nathan. They saw your name on it. They're doubly pissed at you. You were one of their own."

"That doesn't make me a failure," Nathan snapped. "I'm not like you, Cordasic."

"How's Cole?" He decided to push.

"Alive. I'm not a kid killer. Yet. I'm not like you. Everyone knows those kids died because you couldn't talk down the shooter. Just like your partner. I wonder how you live with such a monumental failure every day of your life."

Dom ignored him, focusing on his goal. "Prove you're not a kid killer," he said. "Let Cole go."

"Man, you really do suck as a negotiator," Nathan taunted. "You want me to let the kid go? Then bring me my money." Nathan gave a triumphant laugh. "The clock is ticking." He hung up.

Under his breath, Dom cursed. Round one went to Nathan.

"What happened?" Rachel asked, dropping into the chair next to him. "What did he say?"

"He doesn't want to talk. He wants his money."

"Tell him you've got the two million." Rachel lifted an attaché case.

"Rachel…What have you done?"

Her wide-eyed innocence didn't fool him.

"Did you go the vault?"

Though her face colored, she didn't look away. "Take it."

"What the—" Sebastian began.

Dominic cut him off with a gesture. He took the briefcase from Rachel. "Should I look inside?" he asked her.

She closed her hand over his and leaned in close, close enough for him to smell the vanilla-scented body lotion she wore. "There's nothing in there, Dom. But Nathan won't know that."

Sebastian cursed. "Of all the—"

"Seb, I think Rachel has an excellent idea. I'll take the briefcase in to him. I can negotiate better in person."

And, he didn't say, *try to save Cole, even if it means taking a bullet. Especially if it means taking a bullet.*

Gaze intent, Sebastian slowly nodded. "All right. Call him back and let him know you're coming up. I'll let the authorities know what's going on." He strode over to the assembled group of men and began speaking in a low tone.

Dom picked up the phone, his mouth dry and his chest tight. He couldn't fail. Not this time.

Nathan answered on the second ring.

"What now, Cordasic?" Nathan snarled. "Don't waste my time. I don't want to hear from you unless you're calling to tell me—"

"I am. I have the money. I'd like to personally bring it up."

"Personally?" Nathan chuckled. "Why not? You suck at negotiating, so this might be entertaining. When you get to the door, knock three times. I'll open it, but I'll have my gun to the kid's head. One wrong move, or if I even sniff a sniper outside the door, the kid dies. Understand?" He hung up.

"I understand," Dom said to the empty line. One thing Dom knew—Nathan didn't want to die. And he wouldn't hurt Cole unless he was truly backed into a corner. Cole was his bargaining chip.

"I'll be your backup," Sebastian said. "The Feds say he's in room 2249."

"You stay out of sight. If Nathan sees you, Cole's dead." Without waiting for an answer, Dom turned to go. He didn't look at Rachel, not wanting the distraction. He had to focus on the task at hand and get the situation resolved without any loss of life.

He took the employee elevator to the twenty-second floor. Strode down the carpeted hallway with more confidence than he felt.

Locating room 2249, he tapped three times.

The door slowly opened. Inhaling sharply, Dom stepped inside, letting it slam behind him.

He had three seconds to sum up the situation.

Nathan stood away from the window, large service revolver touching Cole's right temple. Shoulders bowed, head slumped, Cole was tied and gagged.

"Cole," Dom said. "Look at me, buddy."

When the little boy raised his head, his terrified gaze contained a plea. *Help me.*

Eagerness shined in Nathan's eyes. "Where's my money?"

By way of an answer, Dominic lifted the attaché case.

"Hand it over. Now." He held out his other hand. "Slide it across the floor to me. Slowly."

Dom didn't move. "Not until you let Cole go. Untie him."

Nathan's desperate laugh sent an icy chill down Dom's spine. "You're an idiot, Cordasic. Why would I let the kid go? He's my ticket out of here. I've got everything—the money, the list and my precious hostage. You can leave now. I don't need you anymore."

Keeping a firm grip on the briefcase, Dom nodded and turned to go. Though he had no intention of leaving—not without Cole—he wanted Nathan to think he would.

"Leave the money," Nathan barked. "You're more stupid than I thought."

"No." Refusing to rise to the taunts, Dom glanced at his former coworker. With his bloodshot eyes, unshaved jaw, and rumpled clothing, Nathan looked both desperate and dangerous.

A man at the end of his rope.

Though Dom knew good men could turn bad, he knew Nathan. Nathan believed in the FBI creed, heart and soul. So much that he'd frequently been labeled unyielding and hard. He was by the book, right vs. wrong, no gray. For him to have come to this, something or someone had driven him to desperate lengths—so desperate, he was attempting to toss away everything he'd always believed in.

Suddenly something clicked in Dom's mind. Nathan's gambling debts, the threats to Cole to demand the list, desperate attempts to hurt Rachel and Jillie to keep Cole in sight, this crazy kidnapping to demand money to *escape*...

"You poisoned Evan Adair." Of course. Nathan owed money all over the strip. He'd probably become the tool of someone powerful who was on the list—someone who would blackmail a federal agent to guard his secrets. Nathan had been in charge of investigating Evan, undercover, before the man's death; he'd have had countless opportunities to slip Evan poison.

"You can't prove anything," Nathan sneered.

"Gambling losses are a bitch, huh Frederick? Sometimes the only way to pay what you owe is to sell your soul."

Nathan stared, blinking. "None of your business." His mouth twisted and he barked a laugh. "This is your attempt at negotiating the kid's freedom? No wonder Ray got killed."

As taunts went, Nathan had scored a direct hit. But Dom couldn't afford the luxury of reacting. "Give me Cole and I'll give you this briefcase. *This* is my attempt to negotiate. All or nothing, Nathan. Take it or leave it."

Nathan's smile faded as he realized Dom was serious. "You fool. You're willing to risk your girlfriend's son's life? I should call down there and tell her what a loser she sent up."

Dom did the only thing he could—he laughed. "She's not my girlfriend. Now do you want to make the trade or not?"

Desperate he might be. But when push came to shove, Dom didn't think Nathan would hurt Cole. But was he willing to bet Cole's life on it?

"Leave the case." Nathan ordered. "Drop it right this instant or this boy dies."

Ignoring him, Dom once again started for the door. "I'll tell them you didn't want to deal. If I were you, I'd stay away from the windows. Those SWAT snipers are crack shots, even if you have the curtains closed."

When he touched the door handle, Nathan let out a bellow of rage. "I ought to just shoot you right now."

Slowly, Dom turned. "Why don't you?" He pointed to his chest. "Right here, this is my heart. Make it clean and neat so there's not a lot of blood, will you?" He slid his glance to Cole, willing the boy to understand.

Narrow-eyed, Nathan brought the gun around to bear on Dom.

Cole squirmed and pushed himself away. Tied, he fell to the ground and rolled as far as he could from Nathan.

Dominic swung the attaché at Nathan's head. Releasing it, he leapt forward.

Nathan squeezed the trigger. The shot went wild. He shot again and Dom felt a burning in his shoulder, but his momentum carried him forward, on top of Nathan.

He kicked the gun away.

Nathan fought him. With one injured arm, Dom had trouble subduing the smaller man.

The door crashed open. Sebastian and two men in SWAT uniforms charged in, rifles ready.

"No!" Nathan screamed.

Pulling him away from Dom, Sebastian grabbed him, twisting one arm behind, then the other so they could slap on cuffs.

He extended his hand, helping Dom to his feet.

"Thanks."

Sebastian's savage grin matched his expressionless tone. "Don't mention it. What are brothers for?" Grabbing a pillowcase, he tied it tightly around Dom's arm to stop the bleeding. Dom shrugged him away.

Dom went to Cole, removing the gag first, then untying him. He pulled the boy close with his good arm, gratified when Cole wrapped his arms around his neck.

"Are you okay?"

Lower lip trembling, Cole nodded. He sniffled. "I want my mommy."

Lifting him with one arm, Dom carried him to the door. "Then let's go find her."

That night, obviously traumatized, Cole clung to Rachel, finally falling asleep after he finished his dinner. To escape the media crush, Rachel and Jillie had taken refuge in her room. Dom and Seb were still dealing with the authorities. Dom had explained his suspicion that Nathan had killed Evan under duress and then pointed things toward Rachel to give himself time to find the list. No doubt Nathan would be offered a deal to get him to talk.

Dom had declined immediate medical care, calling his shoulder wound a scratch. She imagined he'd get it looked at before retiring for the night.

Rachel planned to find Dom after she finished putting Cole to bed. Not only had he been willing to give his life for her son, but she'd realized one thing in the middle of all this.

Dom was too special for her to let go. She loved him.

Together, they'd find an attorney and fight Evan's will. Surely something could be done to make sure Cole got his rightful inheritance.

Joy bubbled from her heart as she kissed her son's forehead. Tucking him in, she studied him thankfully before turning to rejoin her sister.

"He's sleeping soundly." She closed the door, dropping next to Jillie on the couch. "What a day."

"What do you think is going to happen to Nathan?"

"I'm sure he'll get a fair trial." Rachel tilted her head. "About as fair as he was planning to make sure I got."

Jillie laughed. "At least he doesn't have to worry about the people he owed money killing him. They'll be busy defending themselves now that the FBI has that list."

"True."

"Dom sure was something, wasn't he?"

Rachel beamed. "Yes. Yes, he was."

Jillie looked thoughtful. "You aren't still planning to let him go, are you?"

"Not in a million years." Earnestly, she leaned close and touched her sister's arm. "I never stopped loving him."

"I know. When are you going to tell him?"

Hesitant, Rachel chewed her bottom lip. "I was thinking of telling him now."

"I'll watch Cole. Go to him." Jillie's sympathetic smile bolstered Rachel's confidence. "Try not to botch things up this time, will you?"

Swatting at her sister, Rachel inhaled deeply. "I won't. I just hope he still wants me."

"Oh, believe me, he does. I've seen the way that man looks at you."

Rachel laughed and headed out the door.

When she reached Dominic's suite, he didn't answer the door. She called Dom's cell, but he didn't answer. Her stomach churned. Had he gone to the hospital after all?

Checking with her front desk, she learned the two men had checked out thirty minutes earlier. Her bellman told her they'd taken a cab to the airport for a flight to DFW.

Dom had left without even saying goodbye.

Chapter 13

The late-night flight to Dallas–Fort Worth wasn't crowded. Dom settled into his seat next to the window, opening the magazine he'd purchased at the airport.

Sebastian, who'd been talking on his phone right up until boarding, buckled in beside him.

Sebastian's smile was, as usual, humorless. "Phillip saw you on television again. He must watch a lot in his hospital room. He's ready to see you when we arrive."

Dom refused to allow himself to be moved. Actually he felt numb. Leaving Rachel was not what he'd wanted to do, but what he'd known he *had* to do.

Though his misery felt like an iron weight on his chest, Dom had to laugh. "At least one good thing has come out of all of this. I get to see Phillip before he dies."

"Yeah. Though he didn't say anything about letting you have your inheritance."

"I don't care about the money." Surprisingly, Dom realized he didn't. Of course, he wouldn't have turned down fifty million, but reconciling with Phillip meant more than any dollar amount.

The plane began backing up in preparation for departure. While the flight attendant went over the standard safety instructions, Dom settled back and stared blankly at his magazine. Though by saving Cole he'd proved to himself—and, apparently, his grandfather—that he was still a damn fine hostage negotiator, he felt empty, incomplete. He wondered if he'd ever feel whole again.

"He's gone." Returning to her room, Rachel paced. She couldn't sit still. She felt as if by continually moving, she could keep her heart from cracking wide open. "He and Sebastian left. I think they went to Dallas to see their grandfather. He's in the hospital there."

Jillie's mouth tightened. "I'll have to talk to Sebastian about them just leaving," she said. "I can't believe—" Then she took another look at Rachel's face. Stricken, she shook her head. "I'm sorry."

"It doesn't matter." Rachel waved away the apology. "I didn't even get a chance to tell him I've changed my mind. He's obviously given up on me."

"Go after him," Jillie ordered. "You know the man's crazy about you. I'll stay here with Cole. Do you know what hospital their grandfather's in?"

"I think Dom said Presbyterian in Dallas. But I won't leave Cole. He needs me more than anything right now."

"Let's all go. You can visit Mom while you're there. And

Cole can meet his grandma. That'll take his mind off everything. It'd be great for him."

Her breath caught in her lungs. "You're right. We need to go." She punched a number into the phone. When her personal assistant, Debra, answered, she asked her to make immediate reservations on the next possible flight to Dallas-Fort Worth International Airport. "I'll be down shortly," she concluded.

Jillie beamed at her. "You go, girl."

"Thanks." Hugging her sister, Rachel felt invigorated. "We should pack. If Debra works her usual magic, we'll be landing in Dallas just a few hours behind them."

When Sebastian woke him upon descent, to his shock, Dom realized that he'd fallen asleep. Over two and a half hours had passed.

After their plane touched down at DFW International, they waited until their turn came to disembark. They collected their baggage without speaking and walked outside.

"My car is in long-term parking," Seb said. "If you want to get a rental, I'll bring you back tomorrow."

Weary to the bone, Dom nodded.

Sebastian drove a new black Hummer H2. Impressed, Dom whistled. Seb raised a brow, but didn't comment. They tossed their luggage in back and took off, heading east on Highway 183 toward Dallas.

Staring out his window as the mid-cities flashed past, Dom waited until they'd reached Irving and the old Texas stadium before turning to his brother. "Not much has changed."

"Nope. Not off the freeway, at least."

Though it was late, they went directly to the hospital.

Once they'd parked, Dom turned to his brother. "How bad is he, Seb? Remember, the last time I saw him, he wasn't sick."

"He's dying. You know that. He's thinner, more frail. Though his body looks like he's aged a hundred years since he got sick, his mind is still sharp as ever. So is his tongue."

Dom didn't move. How to explain to his brother that he'd longed for this moment for the past three years and now that it had finally arrived, all he could think about was Rachel.

"Are you ready now?"

At Dom's nod, Sebastian strode off without waiting to see if he followed.

Though visiting hours had ended, the Cordasic family's money granted them special privileges. In the waiting room outside the elevator, a large contingent of family were gathered. Someone had obtained more chairs and lined them up against one wall; it was all reminiscent of a wake.

His aunt Imogene saw him first, gasping. She cried out and enveloped him in a hug. After a moment of startled shock, his other aunts and uncles did the same. His cousins surrounded him, talking about how they'd seen him on the news earlier. He realized that with his shame and his estrangement from Phillip, he'd lost touch with the rest of the family, too.

When everyone finally calmed down, Dom looked around the crowd, searching for two familiar faces. "Where's Mom and Lea?"

Uncle Kenneth harrumphed. "Your mother almost fainted. Lea took her home to get some rest. They said they'd be back first thing in the morning."

"Do you want me to call her?" his cousin Sheila asked.

"Let her sleep. I can wait to see her until tomorrow." He could imagine his mom's reaction. She'd make sure his old bedroom was ready for him and offer to cook his favorite lasagna. And, just like that, he'd be welcomed home.

Blinking, Dom coughed, his throat suddenly tight.

"He's awake." His aunt Edith had just joined them. "I told him you were here and he wants to see you." She pointed to the room, two doors down the hall.

Seb crossed to his side. "Do you want me to go with you?"

"No." Clasping his brother's shoulder to thank him, Dom moved away. "This is something I have to do alone."

Like all hospital rooms, this one was sterile, the furniture utilitarian. Unlike all hospital rooms, there were bright flower arrangements and plants on every available surface.

The shrunken old man in the bed watched silently as Dom approached, breathing in quick, shallow gasps. His skin appeared tight across his skull, giving him an eerie, cadaverous appearance.

"Hello, Grandfather." Despite Seb's warning, Dom was shocked at how Phillip looked. He'd pictured him the way he'd last seen him, old but hearty.

"Dominic," Phillip rasped. "Glad you could come."

Dom gave an awkward nod. "Me, too."

The wizened face cracked an autocratic smile. "Come here and give me a kiss, boy," he ordered.

Dom complied. The elderly man's cheek was cool and felt like parchment.

Phillip reached out and gripped Dom's hand, his fingers like claws. "I won't apologize, you know."

"I didn't expect you to," Dom answered, tensing. Even now, on his deathbed, his grandfather wanted to battle.

But instead of replying, Phillip's eyelids drifted down and his head drooped. Chin on his chest, he dozed.

Dom dropped into the chair beside the bed and watched him sleep.

He must have dozed himself. A tap on the door startled him awake, and he noticed it was morning. Since no one in their large and rowdy family bothered knocking, he figured a nurse needed to do her rounds.

But when the door opened, Dom froze. "Rachel."

"Hello." Standing in the doorway, she looked beautiful and uncertain.

"What are you doing here?" Pushing to his feet, Dom stared at her, his gaze riveted on her face.

"I couldn't let you go." The warmth in Rachel's voice made his heart turn over. "I was wrong."

He made his expression deliberately blank. "Look, I know you're grateful, Rach. You don't have to try and justify anything. I understand. You've done your part. We all can return to our normal lives. Now please, just go away. I can't do this right now."

A soft snore came from the bed.

She stood on the balls of her dancer's feet, as though prepared to run. But she didn't move, her husky voice full of love and certainty and wonder. "Dom, I'm going to fight the will."

"What if you lose?"

"Then I'll give up the inheritance. Cole will be fine without it. Love is what matters. Your love, and the love I know you feel for my son. When I learned you'd been shot…" She bit her bottom lip, her sapphire eyes filling with tears. "I realized how empty both Cole's and my life would be without you."

"Don't do this to me, Rachel." Glancing at Phillip, he saw the elderly man still slept. "Don't say such things unless you really mean them. I don't think I could take you changing your mind again."

"I won't change my mind. I've been a fool. I love you. Adore you." She dropped to her knees in front of him, still not touching him. Gazing down at her in disbelief and wonder, he saw her eyes were full of love. The permafrost lodged in his heart began to melt.

"Evan forced me to leave you right before we were about to marry. He threatened my sister and my mother. I should have gone to you, I know that now, but I was so afraid. So I did as he asked and left you. I've paid for that thousands of times in the seven years since."

She took a deep breath. "I'm ready to rectify that mistake now. This time, I'm asking you. Will you marry me, Dominic Cordasic? Become my husband, my better half and father to my son?"

He didn't move, couldn't move, couldn't speak. Then joy exploded inside him and a rush of humble gratitude that finally, his heart had been made whole.

Pulling her to him, he gave her his answer in a kiss, hot enough to melt metal. "You'd better be sure, Rachel. Because this time, I won't let you go."

Her eyes sparkled. "Oh, I'm sure." And she kissed him back to prove it.

A sound from the doorway made them look up. Glancing at the still-sleeping Phillip, Sebastian entered the room.

"About time you got here, Rachel. But you could have warned me you were bringing your sister. I think the only reason she's not yelling at me is she doesn't want to wake Cole."

She grinned up at him, still held securely in Dom's embrace. "We took the first flight out. We said hello to everyone in the waiting room, but I didn't see you."

"I had to take a private call. I just heard from my contact in the Bureau. Nathan's taking a deal and his confession will clear your name. Though you still took a chance, leaving town." He paused. "I've got a bit of bad news for you. The Feds have frozen Evan's assets. They'll release this info in a press conference tomorrow morning."

"Frozen?" Rachel frowned. "What does that have to do with me? As long as I can keep the Lone Star running, I don't care. I didn't have anything to do with his assets anyway."

Dom exchanged a look with his brother. "Cole's inheritance would come from Evan's assets."

"Right," Sebastian continued. "And since Evan was illegally funneling money into terrorist activities, it looks like Cole's inheritance will be tied up for years. He may never see any of the money, to be honest with you."

Rachel laughed. "Poetic justice, isn't it?"

"It is." Dom kissed her again.

"What will happen to the Lone Star?"

"They'll probably have to keep it running, at least until something's decided. But they'll appoint their own conservator. You won't be allowed to have anything to do with that."

"So I don't have to stay in Vegas?"

"No."

She caught her breath. Dom tightened his arm around her, his heart full. "You'll have to remain there until you're officially cleared of Evan's murder. Then we can live wherever we want."

Again Seb cleared his throat. "Mind cluing me in?"

"Me, too." Awake now, Phillip spoke up, his paper-thin voice quavering. "What is going on here?"

In his arms, Rachel quivered. But she lifted her chin and smiled lovingly up at him before looking at his grandfather. "Dominic has agreed to do me the honor of becoming my husband."

Sebastian threw back his head and laughed. Dom squinted, peering at his brother. He could have sworn he heard true amusement in the sound.

A second later, Seb's blank gaze met his and he wondered if he'd been wrong. "Congratulations," Seb said, then hugged Rachel. "Welcome to the family."

"Thank you."

Phillip harrumphed. "Dominic," he ordered. "Are you so eager to be a fool that you'll let this woman walk all over you again? I saw on the news how your risked your life to save her child. Isn't that enough?"

Arms still around Rachel, Dom drew her close to his grandfather's side. "Without each other, we're only halves of a whole." He explained about Evan and the will. "I completely understand if you want me to leave," he concluded.

"Leave?" Rachel stiffened. "Why would he want you to do that? You just got here."

Dom kissed the side of her neck tenderly. "He blames

you for everything that happened after you left me. Irrational, I know, but—"

"Irrational?" Phillip barked, the effort making him gasp and cough. When he'd finished, he continued glaring at Dom as though Rachel didn't exist. "I had the papers drawn up to write you back into my will. All I need to do is sign them. If you don't send her away, I'll tear them up, understand?" He looked at Rachel. "Dominic will inherit nothing. So if you're after more money, you're out of luck."

Dom realized that his grandfather still thought Rachel had put money over love all those years ago. In his own way, he was protecting Dom. "Money isn't everything, Grandfather. I would have thought you'd have lived long enough to know that. I'm making the same decision I did before—choosing love."

Rachel turned in his arms, hiding her face in his chest. "I had no idea," she murmured. "Dom, I'm so sorry." She looked back at Phillip. "That doesn't matter to me in the least."

Dom gave Phillip a hard look. Mouth pursed, Phillip glared back in challenge. When he didn't speak, Dom sighed and turned Rachel to face the door.

"Are you ready to tell the rest of my family our news?"

She nodded.

Sebastian stepped in front of them. "Let me have the honor of announcing you."

Rachel looked up at Dom. "Humor him," he whispered. "He's been wanting me to be happy for a long, long time."

"And are you?" she whispered back.

His answer was a quick kiss. "Let me prove it to you later."

Aunt Imogene poked her head in the door. "Is everything all right?"

"Yes," Seb answered quickly. "Can you tell everyone to come in here? I have an announcement to make."

"Of course." She hurried off to gather the others.

Phillip grumbled under his breath. No one paid him any attention.

Rubbing his eyes, Cole peered blearily at them. Seeing Dom, he launched himself into the room, barreling into Dom's legs and wrapping his arms around them.

Laughing, Dom picked him up with his good arm, holding him securely while the little boy laid his head trustingly on Dom's shoulder, beaming.

Once everyone had crowded into the small room, Sebastian cleared his throat loudly, making sure he had everyone's attention. "Today, my brother had his heart's desire fulfilled. He got to see his grandfather one last time while also getting proposed to by the love of his life. I'd like to present Dominic and his fiancée, Rachel, and their son, Cole."

Stunned silence met this announcement. Then, as everyone started congratulating them, behind them, Phillip Cordasic himself started clapping.

Stunned, Dominic turned.

"Bravo," Phillip, smiling his shark's smile. "My boy, I'm proud of you. You stood up for what you believed in and had the courage to change what isn't right. You remind me of myself when I was your age. And Rachel, you've shown me all I need to know. Because I now approve of this union, for a wedding gift…" he paused.

The entire family went still, no doubt thinking he would mention his will and Dom's inheritance.

"My wedding gift to you will be staying alive until your wedding." When he'd finished, tears ran down the old man's hollow cheeks. "How soon can you get it done?"

Now the entire room was either crying or on the verge of tears.

"How soon?" Rachel looked up at him.

Sebastian stepped forward. "Very soon, Grandfather. I've got someone on their way to do blood work for a special license. They should be able to get married tonight."

"But my mother." Rachel sounded on the verge of tears herself. "I'd like my mom to be at our wedding, if at all possible."

"Don't worry," Dom said. "If I know my brother…"

"Already done." Sebastian held up a slip of paper. "She's on her way. I've also called Mom and Lea and woken them up. They'll be here shortly." He gave Rachel a meaningful stare. "With a dress for you. I guessed you wore the same size as my sister."

If Rachel's expression was anything to go by, she was as dazed and stunned as Dom. Kissing her cheek, he murmured a quick "I love you."

She whispered, "I love you," back.

"And I've got a tux that should be just about your size," Seb told Dom.

"One thing for sure," Rachel said, glancing around the room at the riot of blooms. "We've got plenty of flowers."

The entire group erupted in laughter.

Phillip clapped again, drawing everyone's anxious attention. "I think I'm going to make it at least one more day. After all, I've got to change my will so you can inherit. You don't have to rush this much."

Dom looked at Rachel, hoping she could read his heart's desire in his eyes.

Rachel looked back, her answer shining bright for him to see. "I don't want to wait," she said.

Chuckling, Phillip nodded. "Then let's get this hospital room ready for a wedding."

* * * * *

Karen Whiddon's CORDASIC LEGACY *miniseries will be back. Keep up to date on the latest releases from Silhouette Romantic Suspense at www.eharlequin.com.*

Meanwhile, don't miss Karen Whiddon's next wonderful story, part of THE PACK *miniseries,* DANCE OF THE WOLF, *available August 2008 from Silhouette Nocturne!*

THOROUGHBRED LEGACY
*The stakes are high when it comes to love,
horse racing, family secrets
and broken promises.*

A new exciting Harlequin continuity series coming soon!
Led by New York Times *bestselling author*
Elizabeth Bevarly
FLIRTING WITH TROUBLE

Here's a preview!

THE DOOR CLOSED behind them, throwing them into darkness and leaving them utterly alone. And the next thing Daniel knew, he heard himself saying, "Marnie, I'm sorry about the way things turned out in Del Mar."

She said nothing at first, only strode across the room and stared out the window beside him. Although he couldn't see her well in the darkness—he still hadn't switched on a light... but then, neither had she—he imagined her expression was a little preoccupied, a little anxious, a little confused.

Finally, very softly, she said, "Are you?"

He nodded, then, worried she wouldn't be able to see the gesture, added, "Yeah. I am. I should have said good-bye to you."

"Yes, you should have."

Actually, he thought, there were a lot of things he should have done in Del Mar. He'd had *a lot* riding on the Pacific Classic, and even more on his entry, Little Joe, but after meeting Marnie, the Pacific Classic had been the last thing on Daniel's mind. His loss at Del Mar had pretty much ended his career before it had even begun, and he'd had to start all over again, rebuilding from nothing.

He simply had not then and did not now have room in his life for a woman as potent as Marnie Roberts. He was a horseman first and foremost. From the time he was a schoolboy, he'd known what he wanted to do with his life—be the best possible trainer he could be.

He had to make sure Marnie understood—and he understood, too—why things had ended the way they had eight years ago. He just wished he could find the words to do that. Hell, he wished he could find the *thoughts* to do that.

"You made me forget things, Marnie, things that I really needed to remember. And that scared the hell out of me. Little Joe should have won the Classic. He was by far the best horse entered in that race. But I didn't give him the attention he needed and deserved that week, because all I could think about was you. Hell, when I woke up that morning all I wanted to do was lie there and look at you, and then wake you up and make love to you again. If I hadn't left when I did—the way I did—I might still be lying there in that bed with you, thinking about nothing else."

"And would that be so terrible?" she asked.

"Of course not," he told her. "But that wasn't why I was in Del Mar," he repeated. "I was in Del Mar to win a race. That was my job. And my work was the most important thing to me."

She said nothing for a moment, only studied his face in the darkness as if looking for the answer to a very important question. Finally she asked, "And what's the most important thing to you now, Daniel?"

Wasn't the answer to that obvious? "My work," he answered automatically.

She nodded slowly. "Of course," she said softly. "That is, after all, what you do best."

Her comment, too, puzzled him. She made it sound as if being good at what he did was a bad thing.

She bit her lip thoughtfully, her eyes fixed on his, glimmering in the scant moonlight that was filtering through the window. And damned if Daniel didn't find himself wanting to pull her into his arms and kiss her. But as much as it might have felt as if no time had passed since Del Mar, there were eight years between now and then. And eight years was a long time in the best of circumstances. For Daniel and Marnie, it was virtually a lifetime.

So Daniel turned and started for the door, then halted. He couldn't just walk away and leave things as they were, unsettled. He'd done that eight years ago and regretted it.

"It *was* good to see you again, Marnie," he said softly. And since he was being honest, he added, "I hope we see each other again."

She didn't say anything in response, only stood silhouetted against the window with her arms wrapped around her in a way that made him wonder whether she was doing it because she was cold, or if she just needed something—someone—to hold on to. In either case, Daniel understood. There was an emptiness clinging to him that he suspected would be there for a long time.

* * * * *

THOROUGHBRED LEGACY
coming soon wherever books are sold!

Thoroughbred *Legacy*

Launching in June 2008

A dramatic new 12-book continuity that embodies the American Dream.

Meet the Prestons, owners of Quest Stables, a successful horse-racing and breeding empire. But the lives, loves and reputations of this hardworking family are put at risk when a breeding scandal unfolds.

Flirting with Trouble

by *New York Times* bestselling author

ELIZABETH BEVARLY

Eight years ago, publicist Marnie Roberts spent seven days of bliss with Australian horse trainer Daniel Whittleson. But just as quickly, he disappeared. Now Marnie is heading to Australia to finally confront the man she's never been able to forget.

The stakes are high when it comes to love, horse racing, family secrets and broken promises.

A new exciting Harlequin continuity series coming soon!

Silhouette®

Romantic
SUSPENSE

*Sparked by Danger,
Fueled by Passion.*

Seduction Summer:
Seduction in the sand…and a killer on the beach.

*Silhouette Romantic Suspense invites you to the hottest
summer yet with three connected stories from some
of our steamiest storytellers! Get ready for…*

Killer Temptation
by Nina Bruhns;
a millionaire this tempting is worth a little danger.

Killer Passion
by Sheri WhiteFeather;
an FBI profiler's forbidden passion incites a
killer's rage,

and

Killer Affair
by Cindy Dees;
this affair with a mystery man is to die for.

Look for

KILLER TEMPTATION by Nina Bruhns in June 2008
KILLER PASSION by Sheri WhiteFeather in July 2008
and
KILLER AFFAIR by Cindy Dees in August 2008.

Available wherever you buy books!

Visit Silhouette Books at www.eHarlequin.com   SRS27586

REQUEST YOUR FREE BOOKS!

2 FREE NOVELS PLUS 2 FREE GIFTS!

Silhouette® Romantic

SUSPENSE

Sparked by Danger, Fueled by Passion!

YES! Please send me 2 FREE Silhouette® Romantic Suspense novels and my 2 FREE gifts (gifts are worth about $10). After receiving them, if I don't wish to receive any more books, I can return the shipping statement marked "cancel." If I don't cancel, I will receive 4 brand-new novels every month and be billed just $4.24 per book in the U.S. or $4.99 per book in Canada, plus 25¢ shipping and handling per book plus applicable taxes, if any*. That's a savings of at least 15% off the cover price! I understand that accepting the 2 free books and gifts places me under no obligation to buy anything. I can always return a shipment and cancel at any time. Even if I never buy another book from Silhouette, the two free books and gifts are mine to keep forever.

240 SDN EEX6 340 SDN EEYJ

Name _____ (PLEASE PRINT)

Address _____ Apt. #

City _____ State/Prov. _____ Zip/Postal Code

Signature (if under 18, a parent or guardian must sign)

Mail to the **Silhouette Reader Service:**
IN U.S.A.: P.O. Box 1867, Buffalo, NY 14240-1867
IN CANADA: P.O. Box 609, Fort Erie, Ontario L2A 5X3

Not valid to current subscribers of Silhouette Romantic Suspense books.

Want to try two free books from another line?
Call 1-800-873-8635 or visit www.morefreebooks.com.

* Terms and prices subject to change without notice. N.Y. residents add applicable sales tax. Canadian residents will be charged applicable provincial taxes and GST. This offer is limited to one order per household. All orders subject to approval. Credit or debit balances in a customer's account(s) may be offset by any other outstanding balance owed by or to the customer. Please allow 4 to 6 weeks for delivery. Offer available while quantities last.

Your Privacy: Silhouette is committed to protecting your privacy. Our Privacy Policy is available online at www.eHarlequin.com or upon request from the Reader Service. From time to time we make our lists of customers available to reputable third parties who may have a product or service of interest to you. If you would prefer we not share your name and address, please check here. ☐

SRS08

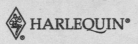

Silhouette®
Romantic
SUSPENSE

COMING NEXT MONTH

#1515 PROTECTING HIS WITNESS—Marie Ferrarella
Cavanaugh Justice

Having left medicine, Krystle Maller is shocked to find a man lying unconscious on her doorstep. She's been in hiding from the mob since witnessing a murder. She fears her discovery might get her—or him—killed, yet she treats her handsome patient. While a gunshot wound may slow him down, undercover cop Zack McIntyre is skilled at protecting the innocent. And he certainly won't let Krystle handle a dangerous threat on her own....

#1516 KILLER TEMPTATION—Nina Bruhns
Seduction Summer

Finding a dead man at the start of her dream job is Zoe Conrad's worst nightmare. But when the man proves to be very much alive—plus charming, filthy rich and sexy as all get out—Zoe knows she's in even more trouble. Giving in to Sean Guthrie's incendiary seduction could be her worst mistake yet. Because while Sean claims to know nothing about the serial killer who's stalking couples on the beach, local authorities have their eyes on Sean and Zoe…and so might a murderer.

#1517 SAFE WITH A STRANGER—Linda Conrad
The Safekeepers

On the run with nowhere to hide, Clare Chandler would stop at nothing to protect her child. Army Ranger Josh Ryan has spent his life hiding from his true identity and relates to the way Clare keeps herself guarded when he rescues her and her son from her ex's henchmen. In order to help them, however, he must face his family and the truth of who he really is…while withstanding his fiery attraction to Clare.

#1518 DANGEROUS TO THE TOUCH—Jill Sorenson

Homicide detective Marc Cruz doesn't care for second-rate con artists—especially those claiming they have psychic powers and a lead on his serial-killer case. Although Marc intends to expose Sidney Morrow for the hoax she is, her impressions—about the investigation and his attraction to her—are proving all too true.

SRSCNM0508